978-1-7393584-1-9

*For all the children I have taught who made this book possible.*

*The stories are true but the names of those involved have been changed.*

# Introduction

Welcome to the diary of a teacher. I am that teacher, Felicity Youngwood. In the epitome of the teacher cliché, I had always wanted to be a teacher. Actually, that's not true. I had at one point wanted to be a dancer, a police officer, a chef, a model and an actress. Goodness knows I'm dramatic enough to be an actress, but I figured it was unlikely to happen and I gave up easily. But teaching! It looked like such a fun job, creative and varied, with lots of room for career progression. I could work anywhere in the country, in the world if I wished with a teaching degree! Oh the lives I would touch, the minds I would nurture, the parents I would support, the creativity I would foster. Except that all I heard from family, friends, strangers and comedians was "oooh you'll get so many holidays" or "oh so you're going to play from 9 'til 3, that's easy". People sure did have a different view of teachers than I did and I still want to hide at a comedy gig as primary teachers always seem to be easy prey. "You work bloody hard, don't you teachers? Half the year, five hours a day." Thanks, Jimmy Carr, you full timer you.

I was determined nonetheless and adamant that I was going into it for the children, though let's face it, the holidays were a pretty peachy bonus. Reading back through the diary of my first year was…interesting. First of all, what grown-ups write diaries? Was it a bit 'cringe' or 'lame' (not sure what the kids say nowadays) to do that? Second of all, but unrelated to this line of points, I use the terms 'grown up' and 'adults' as if talking about people other than myself. I once asked my Gran when she ended up feeling like a grown up because I kept waiting for it to happen and she said at 87 years old she still felt twenty-one. That must have been a surprise every time she looked in the mirror but it's nice to know I'm not the only one who feels or has felt like a fraud! Third of all…was there a third point? This happens a lot, I'll come back to it when it comes back to me. Oh right, writing a diary. Thirdly, I was struck by how my attitudes had changed over the decade or so I had been working as a teacher and how I promised myself things in my first year that I wouldn't ever do or say or become. I often managed to remind myself of these but sometimes, you end up muttering to yourself how much you hate children (when you absolutely don't) or how you desperately need a holiday (when it's only been three weeks since the last one) or how...well, let's see shall we.

# Contents Page

# Chapter 1
# Autumn term 1

**Monday 24th August**

Most people will start a diary on the first of January. New year, new you, and all that nonsense. The trouble is, when you've just come out of education and now have a job in education, January isn't really the start of a new year. It's the start of the second term in a school year. So I'm starting my diary now.

Today, was my first day in my new school as a teacher. I'd been in before, for my interview and to meet my class, but it didn't really count because I was escorted round and there was already a class and teacher in what would eventually be my classroom. But when I went in today to set it up, as it's during the summer holidays, the whole school was empty. Silent. Creepy really. You expect to hear children's voices or the three consecutive claps of an adult trying to get the attention of thirty feral mini humans, but today there was nobody else there. I guess they all picked a different day to go into their classrooms so it was just me. Thank goodness, because I got stuck in the art cupboard. Not locked in, actually physically stuck.

I'd learned through all my placements that teaching cupboards are often like the cupboards under the stairs that people have at home. Everything looks so tidy in the room, but you open that cupboard and your whole life falls on top of your face after months of just shoving random odds and ends in there that didn't have a proper home. It's apparently the same at school. Extra exercise books; cupboard. Confiscated toys you forgot to return; cupboard. The class camera that doesn't work; cupboard. I guess it's hard enough to keep your own classroom cupboard in working order, never mind the communal ones. There must not be enough time to put a tray back on the shelf that's right in front of you so it's just dumped in the middle of the floor with the aim to sort it out another time, but it's never done and it all piles up. The adult sized chairs were in there ready for assemblies, the stage stacked in a corner ready to come out for Christmas and there's an infuriating beeping coming from the tray of stopwatches.

So I found myself picking my way through the 'art' cupboard (a not-altogether accurate name as it housed all of the aforementioned items plus many more topic boxes that no-one teaches anymore but who knows when you'll need a Roman artefact in the future? Better keep it just in case). I needed to get to the back to get some coloured card, when my foot got wedged. The trouble was, I was in a pretty wide stance that I was assuming momentum would carry me through.
So I had no leverage. I tried to bend down to free my foot with my hands but nearly fell over. I remember having a Wii Fit at one point and it gets you to do an initial assessment before you start exercising with it. During the balance assessment it asked me if I fall down a lot! How rude! A machine called me clumsy! The trouble is, this cupboard escapade may have proven it right.

Anyway, I got my phone out of my back pocket and text my mum "I'm stuck in the art cupboard". Apparently, she laughed so hard she couldn't reply for a little while; not altogether helpful but it gave me some thinking time. Not practical thoughts, like just look down and wiggle your foot out, or what can I grab onto to pull myself free. Thoughts like, I wonder if this is how mice feel when they get stuck in traps, and, has anyone else been stuck in this cupboard? Eventually I managed to haul myself out, leaving behind my shoe and falling particularly ungracefully into some boxes of clay. Stupid gravity.

The moral of the story is, being as clumsy as I am, I shouldn't venture into strange, full cupboards alone.

**Tuesday 25th August**

I went back to school today and managed to not get stuck anywhere – this is a big achievement! I was moving my classroom around and immediately regretted moving the desk. Note to self; must work out more. I knew I wanted to put the Lego out for the children's first day (mostly because I wanted to play with it) but I had to spend ages looking around everything else to find out what was there, reorganise it and then decide what to put out. Reception is going to be awesome and as it turns out, there will be a lot of playing in my future career – winner! In the end, I went for Lego, dolls house (quite a large spider in there, it'll either move on or I'll let the kids deal with that one), some jigsaws, colouring and lots of other environmentally apocalyptic plastic games. I spent the whole day in my classroom, forgot to eat and came home absolutely covered in dust, but I am so happy! I must've spent my year's budget on printing and laminating already, but nobody else was there so it's ok. Sorry environment. According to the Year One teacher back in July, you hide away the laminating pouches, book stickers and other allocated stationary items, never lend anyone anything and always ask for more when the order form comes round.

Apparently, teaching has some similarities to being a bandit.

**Wednesday 26th August**

I had one last day in school before term starts next week. I think I have PTSD from the art cupboard, I still get nervous walking through the hall and hearing the threatening beep of that rogue stopwatch. Turns out, I didn't have a lot to do so I just came back home. I had a lunchtime fruity cider (because I don't yet drink actual adult drinks like beer, red wine or coffee) and had a little afternoon nap. Good day.

**Monday 31st August**

My Dad called today to wish me luck for starting work tomorrow, he's so thoughtful. He has so much confidence in me and I am really excited, but my stomach won't stop doing flips. I'm so nervous. We've got two inset days before the children start but I'm not sure if that makes it better or worse. What if I'm rubbish? What if the staff all sit in little cliques for the inset days and I don't belong with anyone so I have to sit by myself? The last few days have been so lovely sitting in the garden, soaking up the last bit of time I had being technically unemployed, but now the dread and the fear are setting in and I'm not sure I'll be able to sleep tonight!

**Tuesday 1st September**

It's official, I am a teacher! I have my ID badge, with my ever so slightly terrified smile, my computer log in, with a password I almost immediately forgot, and my very first INSET day under my belt! What a day. I mean, let's be honest, it was an awful start to my teaching career. Two hours of safeguarding where you look at all the faces of children who have died in the last ten years to ensure we know what to look out for, then two hours of going through the handbook, policies and a refresher on how unacceptable last year's data was. No pressure, but make it better this year! Yikes. There were sweets on the table, though, (lemon sherbets! I wondered aloud if Dumbledore would be joining us but nobody else seemed to get it) so that was alright. It was a bit awkward, knowing who to sit with and making small talk with strangers, especially because everyone already knows each other and I keep trying to jump on other people's conversations – oh you went to Cornwall, how lovely! Dweeb. It's that really strange feeling of being surrounded by people whilst at the same time feeling quite isolated. People were really kind and the phase leader took me round again to make sure I knew where everything was.

Being in a whole room full of people is not my strength. I've been getting more pronounced social anxiety as I get older and this was really difficult, but I know they are going to end up being my work family from now on. I assume this means I will like some of them, dislike but tolerate some of them and never speak to others. I'm also not sure I like the term work family. I might not use that one again. I'm very socially tired from today.

**Wednesday 2nd September**

My teaching assistant (TA) is terrifying. She is called June Clark and she's at least 106 years old. She has long, wild, curly grey hair and doesn't seem to do anything at less than 60mph. She wasn't in yesterday because she had some sort of appointment so I only met her today. She welcomed me to the school but her smile didn't quite reach her eyes and I immediately wondered if she's ever killed anyone. This is a bit dramatic, but she strikes me as the kind of person who could get away with it. I'll have to take her some biscuits. Biscuits would definitely make her like me. She has, however, worked at the school for 97 years, so she knows absolutely everything. I bet she can pick her way through the nightmare that is the art cupboard without getting stuck in it. Gravity wouldn't dare sabotage her. She showed me where the good cake is kept in the staff room and taught me how to use the photocopier, though I'm pretty sure she only knows how to do two things on it so this will be awkward when I know more than her. Is that arrogant? Assuming that I'll be better than someone else at something because she's ancient? Well, we'll see won't we. Youth against...well...age.

The children are starting tomorrow and I'm not sure how to feel! I'm nervous and excited and doubting myself and trying to give myself a pep talk all at the same time. I can do this. I've been trained for this. This isn't war. It's just children. Someone somewhere is muttering 'famous last words'.

**Thursday 3rd September**

I was so excited when I got up this morning. I went racing in at 7.30am to make sure everything was set up and that I'd got my laminating pouches squirrelled away. My terrifying TA (now to be nicknamed TTA because using her actual name doesn't seem to convey the right level of how scary she is to me) came in about half 8 and I mostly hid from her while she flew around sorting things that I didn't even know needed sorting. As I started to watch the children and their parents start filing into the playground I had a sudden thought. I'd done three years of university learning and six teaching practices, but never before had I done a first day. What the hell happens on a first day? What if they don't listen to me? What if someone breaks their leg? What if I forget to feed them? What if what if what if. What happens when, how do I, where is...all the questions I'd had six weeks to ask flooded my brain and I couldn't seem to remember my own name. This was a terrible idea. Thirty children. Thirty! Four and five years old. Did I mention there are thirty of them? Just me and TTA. Still, the bell rang, as I knew it would (however hard I've tried I have learned that I cannot control things with my mind...must stop watching programmes like Charmed) and for the first time, I arranged my face into the biggest grin possible without making myself look like an insane Cheshire cat and I opened the door...

It was very gentle chaos! My panic about being left alone with thirty children wasn't necessary because there were actually only fifteen of them. With it being their first day of 'proper' school, we had half in the morning and half in the afternoon. There was some pretty intense crying from two of them after twenty minutes when they turned round from the water tray to realise that their parents had gone. Wow they can really cry! I've never hugged such a wet person before. I might need to bring a change of clothes in with me if this is an indication of how teaching Reception will be! As it turns out, TTA has a lovely soft side to her and scooped the criers up and distracted them with such ease that I'm pretty sure I was staring at her with my mouth open for far too long.

The children and parents are all so lovely. There were also a couple of parent criers who tried to pass it off as sneezing. There was one who I was sure was going to start banging on the window yelling 'look at me, love me!' but he managed to restrain himself. The windows have got a lovely film on them so that we can see out easily but, depending on the light, you can't see in unless you press your face up against the window, which every one of the parents succeeded in not doing. It's quite lovely actually, after seeing so many parents on Facebook just willing the school term to start so that their kids could pop back off for five days a week.

I was really proud of myself for learning most of the children's names by the end of each session, but handover is so scary! Not only do you have to learn the children's names, but also the faces of one, two, three or sometimes four different adults who might at some point be collecting that child from school. One lady was in a proper rush and started yelling "Clarence! Clarence!" even though she could see that I had a line of children who were going out in order one at a time. She's going to be interesting. TTA was again a fantastic help and went out into the playground to chat while I sorted out who was going home with whom and she managed to point out the one at a time lining up system to this particular parent!

Most of the day was a blur but some things I do know:

1. Nobody got hurt.
2. TTA is a kick-ass cry-stopper.
3. I survived my first day as a teacher.
4. I already miss afternoon naps.

**<u>Friday 4th September</u>**

More children cried today. More! We had loads of great games set up and I'm really fun so I didn't really understand it. Come on kid, just play with this Lego and your whole life is suddenly outstanding! I got really carried away with some colouring I was doing and had to remind myself that I was supposed to be there in a working capacity, but it's all good mental health for us all... All of this, however, cannot compete with the fact that for the last six weeks, these children have been home with their parents and I think it started to set in on them today that that's over. They start full time next week and I'm not too proud to say...I'm worried about the criers!

I learned a lot from TTA yesterday, though. Distraction is the best medicine! I had a great time reading loads of stories to them and my heart swelled up like the Grinch's when a couple of others heard and came over, crawling into my lap or snuggling up next to me. Cute! That really helped the ones who were upset, as did songs and rhymes. There's a gorgeous home video of my sister when she was about 3 singing Wind The Bobbin Up, so we did that over and over in different voices and different speeds – doing the fast version had everyone rolling around laughing!

On the other hand, Terrence was caught spitting in the sand pit. You can't win them all.

**Saturday 5th September**

I know it probably won't always be like this, but considering it was only the first week and I didn't have any marking or sticking photos in their learning journeys and the planning for the next week is done, I'm just having a lovely weekend! It's my friend's birthday next week so we went out for brunch, which always feels very grown up even though I invariably having pancakes covered in sweet stuff like a child. I avoided Mum for much of the afternoon so that I wouldn't have to go to a garden centre with her (I'm not green fingered at all and have no desire to traipse round a bunch of plants at the weekend, though she laughs and assures me that'll change… we'll see) so I watched some rubbish TV and ate too much chocolate and generally had a lovely time!

Is it too early to think that this teaching life is just marvellous?

**Sunday 6th September**

I went to Snobs last night, a club in Birmingham that we used to go to all the time when we were about 17/18, and good Lord was it sticky in there. We went in once to watch Less Than Jake, a band I genuinely adore, and I callously dismissed a guy who was asking me for a cigarette thinking he was hitting on me, but when he turned round and walked back into the VIP area I actually looked at him and realised he was one of the band and I've never been able to get over that. So now, I'm always alert for this but it's obviously never happened since.

Mum made me a hangover sausage sandwich this morning like the absolute legend that she is and we spent a bit of time house hunting for me online. My eyes are way bigger than my budget so I often need reigning in. I'm sending any potentials to Dad for his opinion too, my parents are so knowledgeable and worldly I'm not sure I'll ever be able to make a life decision without their input! Though when they disagree with me my thoughts on that change...

**Monday 7$^{th}$ September**

Good Lord! Thirty children compared to fifteen is loud! So loud! Most of them are settling in to my three-clap attention strategy but a couple of them give me a side eye like they're thinking "you clap away, I'm far too busy and important with burying this pencil in the sand for whatever it is you want to announce". Luckily TTA is on the case and one swift look from her gets them standing to attention! It's powerful. I need to work on my teacher look. I need that look.

They all stayed all day today, which includes lunch and lots of them were petrified of the hall. TTA and I stayed with them while they ate and I had to take my lanyard off because when I leant over them to cut their chicken up, it kept smacking them in the face. Is it wrong that I found it quite amusing? They need to develop survival skills, right? At the same time, I probably don't want to injure anyone with a plastic photo of my face so I need to remember that going forwards.

I did, however, achieve a little win in the form of getting the Phonics baseline assessments done. I remember starting my first placement and someone mentioning Phonics and I had zero idea what the hell they were talking about! Turns out, it's basically learning to hear, say, recognise and write sounds in order to read and write. Simple enough, right?

To be fair, doing the initial assessments to see what their exiting knowledge is wasn't too difficult. Most children didn't really know much, which is a great place to start seeing as, as Julie Andrews would advise us, we'll be starting at the very beginning anyway. There are some children who already know some sounds, but mostly if they recognise a letter it's by its' name. There are the lovely ones who just stared at me blankly the whole time, bless them. I had one hilarious interaction with Badra who doesn't speak very much English. it went something like this:

"Badra, what's the first sound you can hear in sit?"

"G."

"Ooh good try, it's not g, listen again. S-it."

"G."

"Well done for trying, remember it's not g. Listen to the start of the word again. Ssssss-it." Here I started to really draw out the s.

"G."

This back and forth went on for a little while until I gave up saying the word altogether and was just hissing a long 's' sound at her.

"Sssssssssssssss..."

"G."

"Sssssssssssssss..."

"G."

I felt like screaming! NO! IT'S NOT G! We called it quits and went our separate ways. Let's hope that gets better.

**<u>Tuesday 8th September</u>**

Ok. Let's just talk about the smells. All the smells. Especially now that they're staying all day, that carpet time after lunch is RIPE. They all find it hilarious, of course, but my nostrils are personally offended. I had to nip out to the outdoor area at one point for some fresh air and had a chat with the TA from the next-door class. She's absolutely hilarious! She told me she loved working with children, especially the smelly ones, because you could blame anything on them! She said she could walk into a classroom for a few seconds, supposedly talk to a child or pick up a book, then walk back out, all the while letting one go that others would then blame on the children. I wondered if TTA did that...I wouldn't dare question her about it so maybe she's got a great cover and every time I think there's a child omitting a stink it's actually her! Either way, I need to buy some air fresheners.

**Wednesday 9th September**

This is tiring work. My Dad keeps asking me if I'm having a lovely time getting paid to play with children from 9-3 every day. I tried to explain that I get in at 7.30 and don't leave until at least 5pm and it's not all playing, but he just chuckles and mutters something about 'not a real job'. Hmm. I shall reflect this level of respect in his Christmas present this year.

We're trying to get carpet time down. I've given them carpet spaces, TTA changed a couple and I didn't dare challenge her or ask for reasons, and we're trying to get them to remember which animal butt they have to sit on. Yep! The carpet has a variety of animals with their butts facing out for the children to sit on! I didn't notice at first but it's a great idea.

The trouble is, Francisco is scared of elephants, Phillipa keeps making monkey noises when she sits on the monkey space, Gary wants to sit wherever Gary wants each time and Imran keeps repeating everything I say to her giraffe. Giving children a space to sit in is not something I had ever anticipated having to try very hard at but between those who can't remember their animal and those who just don't want theirs, it takes us all five minutes just to sit down! I have barely been able to start any formal teaching as by the time we've got everyone sorted, those who just come and sit down immediately have already got ants in their pants from being sat for too long.

People have been telling me for years that children are like sponges and soak up new information quicky. This is not true of remembering an animal butt.

I'm going to tackle Phonics tomorrow.

**Thursday 10th September**

I'll try Phonics tomorrow.

**Friday 11th September**

Yesterday was one royal shit show. Literally! It was just one of those days when everything went wrong. Aryani came walking out of the toilets with their pants round their ankles shouting "I'm done!" – apparently Aryani does not self-wipe at home. That was an interesting encounter and a fun conversation with parents, who were apparently oblivious to the fact that me and TTA were not employed to provide that level of personal care to 30 four-year-olds all day every day.

Then later on that morning, poor Kem got an upset stomach whilst outside. He ran all the way through the garden and through the length of the classroom, dripping diarrhoea as he went, finally managing to reach the toilets and somehow projecting it over the walls and floor. Now, for all of the wonderful, proactive, knowledgeable aspects there are to TTA, she cannot deal with poo. She very quickly left the classroom and stood outside the door in the corridor, peering in through the window as I cleaned Kem up, mopped the whole bathroom, mopped the classroom floor, hosed down the path outside and tried to keep my eye on the other 29 children, whilst trying not to be sick. Poor Kem was mortified and obviously pretty poorly, but funnily enough, four-year-olds don't have that level of empathy yet and just kept going on about the smell! To be fair to them, it was still lingering today.

So whilst we managed to do some fun counting on the carpet in the morning, Phonics did not materialise due to the all the poo.

Today was a bit calmer though, and we managed to get them sat in their carpet spaces atop the correct animal butts relatively quickly without much opposition, so we managed to do some listening games. We'll start learning letter sounds next week so I'm brushing up on what phonemes and graphemes are, yikes!

I'm so happy it's Friday. I've had a really great first couple of weeks but the mental capacity you need to take care of thirty small children all day every day is incredible. Teachers are superhumans. Fact.

Is it normal for grownups to go to bed at 9.30pm on a Friday night?

**Saturday 12th September**

I'm so tired. I couldn't tell you what I did today or at any point what time it was. I definitely spoke too quickly last weekend.

**Sunday 13th September**

My Mum, my sister Diane (Di) and I went over to see our Grandparents today (Mum's parents). I remember telling a friend at university that I was going to see them one weekend, and their response was something like "Oh no, you poor thing, can't you get out of it?" I didn't understand this at all, until they explained that their Nan is quite tough and a bit mean and their Grandpa is just beaten down. My Grandparents are nothing like this; they're absolutely glorious. They've been together since they were teenagers, they still laugh and joke and play together and my Uncle lives with them; the three of them have such hilarious little bits and the six of us together are just the best group. They take us on holiday every year, we often spent some of our school holidays with them and since I can remember we've been seeing them every few Sundays.

My Grandad has the cheekiest grin and the longest legs. He'll often clip you under the table with his foot or his walking stick and claim that you're in his space, to which we have a fun little argument about. He tells fantastic stories about growing up seeing the gas man turning the street lamps on and will always lose a battle against Di about who gets the skin of the custard.

My Gran is so smart and fun, but watch out if you're ever on her bad side, because she has sharp little fingers that nip your skin on your arm or leg and it really hurts! When she looks up at my Grandad when they go to kiss, she often spies a cobweb out of the corner of her eye and rushes off to get the duster, leaving Grandad smooching the air in front of him wondering what on earth happened!

My Uncle is wonderful. He used to let us push him the pool fully clothed when we were on holiday and bury him in the sand. He's got a really ticklish neck and an intense aversion to sour sweets, so of course we like to touch his neck and feed him sour fizzy sweets!

I didn't get as much time with my Dad's parents. His Dad died when I was ten and we lost his Mum a few years ago too. We've got fantastic home videos and I love to hear his hearty laugh and her northern accent (we're all Yorkies). I'm sure there was a point where I got a bit too cool to be hanging out with my grandparents, but I love our family Sundays now. It often makes me think about the time we did have with my other Grandparents before they passed and how Dad still gets more northern whenever he's around or talking to one of his seven siblings!

**Monday 14th September**

Today. Was. Awesome! The thing with this school is, each half term you teach through a topic, and at the beginning of each topic you have a theme day, where you all dress up and do fun activities to introduce the theme to the children for the half term to get them excited. Tick! Excitement levels peaked! Our theme for this half term (that I got from the previous planning, thank you very much) is Plenty of Pirates. TTA and I stayed so late on Friday and came in so early this morning to change up the room so it looks like a pirate island. There are hanging nets, gold medallions (that I'm sure will get shoved into pockets and drawers so fast!), huge fabric flags and even a cardboard cut out pirate ship! The place looks insane, I genuinely want to play in it.

Also, yes, I went to work today dressed up as a pirate! I have to say, I suit it quite well. I know women didn't used to be pirates so much as they were 'wenches', stupid misogyny, but I would've made an awesome looking pirate! I did lots of tiny curls to make my hair huge (channelling Dustin Hoffman from Hook), drew scars and a moustache on my face with eyeliner, and my costume came with a particularly suave-looking hat complete with feather! I didn't go too mad with the eye make-up as I didn't want to scare the children out of coming into the room, but good God TTA gave it some umph! She barely broke character all day, though I suppose being naturally terrifying gave her a pirate-y edge. She even brought a hook to wear over her hand for the day and managed to keep it on longer than I would've! New respect for TTA.

We had an awesome pirate party with pirate themed food and games, including walk the plank (a wooden bench), mutiny (a bit like what's the time Mr Wolf?) and a treasure hunt, as well as loads of pirate-themed art and craft stations. It was so much fun!

I wasn't quite prepared for the amount of parents (and children, but they're more forgivable) who openly and without restraint, laughed in my face today! Granted, I was sporting a superb fake moustache, but I thought my efforts deserved a round of applause rather than mocking.

I'm pretty sure that you can call this theme officially introduced, and that the children are well and truly pumped for learning. I am knackered though, and it's only Monday!

## Tuesday 15th September

It is incredible how fast thirty children can decimate a fantastically set up classroom! Poor TTA and I were devastated within about fifteen minutes of them going off to their activities this morning! It's so funny how you have a vision of how things should be set up and played with as an adult, yet children won't share that vision with you. They just wanted to destroy everything. The whole class spent about twenty minutes before lunch and before the end of the day getting things back to where they started. I wonder if that's a lesson to learn for them or for me. Maybe the gold coins didn't need to stay in the role play area and perhaps putting the pirate figures from the sand into the water tray was genius. I might need to learn to be a bit more flexible and go with where the children take the learning, but still, ripping apart the giant carboard pirate ship shouting 'bombs away' isn't exactly respecting property!

We managed to start Phonics this morning, though (I figured a room full of pirates probably wouldn't be sitting to learn a letter sound yesterday!) and it went pretty well. There's some Phonics songs online, which are super cute, plus a guy using a hand puppet to find things around his house starting with the letter you're learning. We put s' everywhere! They were in the sand tray, the water tray, the creative station, in the role play pirate den – everywhere! Badra did much better today having learnt the right sound, she is no longer saying 'g' at me while I hiss in her face. Progress!

## Wednesday 16th September

I've started getting my non-contact time this week. Every teacher is entitled to 10% of their weekly contracted hours for planning, preparation and assessment (hence PPA) and as a Newly Qualified Teacher (NQT) for the first year I get an extra 10% of non-contact time. 10% amounts to around half a day and it's particularly delicious because my school have allocated both of these to a Wednesday, so I get the whole day out of class! It seems strange to be so excited to teach but also be so excited for a whole day away from the children, but there is just so much paperwork to do outside of actual teaching that it's amazing to get time to do it. Plus, teaching is tiring! Being with people and talking all day, dealing with behaviour issues, trying to keep up with the pace of the curriculum; it's all a lot to deal with, so a mid-week break is just lovely. I think I'll still pop over in the morning when they're arriving at school and maybe at the end of the day when they go home. I'm not sure if that's me being conscientious or controlling. We'll see I suppose!

The only difficulty is that non-contact time is taken in the staff room. I've eaten more biscuits today than I ate all of last week. This is going to be a problem.

**<u>Thursday 17th September</u>**
It's Jeans For Genes day tomorrow; raising money for genetic disorders just by bringing a pound in for the pleasure of wearing your jeans to school. This is revolutionary! I've set an alarm to remind myself as I don't want to be the goober who turns up in anything but jeans when you can actually wear jeans to work. This is a big week for dressing up, the parents must have spent so much money on their uniforms and then straight away there are two days in a week where they don't even have to wear them!

In other news I sneezed whilst doing the register this morning. Here's the conversation that followed:
Mehmet - "What are you doing, Miss Youngwood?"
Me - "Sneezing, Mehmet."
Mehmet – "Oh."
Scintillating huh.

Also, 9.30pm has officially become my bed time.

**<u>Friday 18th September</u>**

Jeans For Genes day. I shouldn't be so excited about having been allowed, no, encouraged to wear jeans to work but I was delighted! The trouble is, so were the children. Their energy levels were through the roof, just like Monday when they came in dressed as pirates so I'd been prepared today; I lowered the lights ever so slightly and put some calming music on the whiteboard with a video of a tranquil sea, but none of them heard or saw any of it because they were all just running around like maniacs! Jeeeeeeeeeans!

It's so funny how different they all look out of their uniform too, it took me a while to fully recognise some of them! I just felt so bad for the ones whose parents hadn't read the letter or had forgotten and came wearing their uniforms. Four-year-olds don't have the grace to ignore a mistake and were all over these little ones, peppering them for information as to why they didn't wear their jeans to school. We had to have another little chat about empathy but we'll need to work on this more!

**Saturday 19th September**

Ah internet dating. I met a guy in a pub who barely spoke two words to me. At one point, I was babbling on about whether rattan furniture shrinks in the rain or not to fill the silence and he literally just got up and walked off! I got my phone out to ask Mum if I could just leave, but he came back with another drink each for us. It. Was. Painful.

**Sunday 20th September**

I took Mum to see a flat with me today. I was so excited. It's in Catherine-de-Barnes and from the lounge window, through some tiny gaps in the other buildings surround the flat, you could see fields! I was all set to buy it but Mum wasn't excited and when I spoke to Dad about on the phone later he agreed. On reflection, the flat was tiny and overpriced due to its location.

They are wise people, my parents. It's both useful and infuriating.

**Monday 21st September**

I feel like I've mostly got to grips with teaching children. I'm still learning, obviously, but I've found a really good balance between being firm and strict without being horrible or shouty. We're having a great time together and they're slowly starting to understand my sense of humour, though I think this will take more time! The parents, however, still make me nervous. I'm still learning who they all are, though I can match them up with the right child now, no problem, and I've got a pretty good handle on the ones who I can share a joke with and the ones I need to be really careful with what I say to them or how I say it.

Tonight was curriculum evening, where all the parents for Nursery and Reception came to hear about the school's Early Years curriculum, data, assessments, trips and other school news. I had to stand up with the phase leader and talk through a couple of the slides and I could barely breathe I was so nervous! You know when you can hear that someone is inhaling but not exhaling the whole way? That was me. Shaking like a leaf. I suppose I was the same when the children first started, but I'm a bit more used to them and I can blag whatever I don't know because...well they're four, they don't know! Adults, however. Adults know. I just deflected all of the comments to the phase leader who's worked in Early Years for years and wow does she know her stuff! I know I'll have to deliver parent workshops and eventually assemblies where parents might be there so I'll have to get used to it, but the children seem to really enjoy my silliness and that doesn't seem to be the way I'm going to win over the parents that I'm the best person to teach their children...

It made it such a long day. Arriving at 7.30am and leaving the school at 7.15pm. I need more snacks next time I do this, I can't keep eating the amount of biscuits from the staff room that I have been, I'm sure my trousers are already getting a bit tighter.

**Tuesday 22nd September**

It's happening. Freshers' Flu. I know I'm not at university but it still appears to be a thing! Half of the children have been ill already, all snuffly and snotty, and I woke up to the joys of a sore throat this morning, like I'm swallowing broken glass. Do you want to know what isn't a good remedy for a headache and a throat so sore you can barely whisper? Thirty children.

**Wednesday 23rd September**

A parent said to me this morning "ooh are you still poorly? You look dreadful!" Bitch.

**Thursday 24th September**

Oh my goodness I feel awful. I don't want to call in sick because I've barely been here a minute, but I don't know how I even got through the day. This must be how parents feel when they are poorly and have children still needing to be fed and loved and looked after, except in this case there's a million of them.

**Friday 25th September**

I barely had any voice today. I wonder if people with office jobs find it easier to work while they're poorly if they can avoid talking to people all day, or if that's an idiot assumption of someone who hasn't done that job before. I'm going to load up on vitamins and then spend the weekend in bed I think.

**Saturday 26th September**

Bleurgh. Can't.

**Sunday 27th September**

We went back over to my Grandparents' today for my Uncle's birthday. It was a gorgeous day so we went out to Bradgate Park for a walk in the afternoon. The fresh air was lovely but I still wasn't feeling well at all, so crashed pretty hard again this evening from expending so much energy. But it's always so fun to see them and we had a delicious roast and a choosing tea in the evening; basically we put all the components of a sandwich out on the table and you can make yourself a ploughman's!

Bradgate Park is so great. We used to go a lot as kids and there's areas with huge ferns growing, so Di and I used to play hide and seek in them. In the summer when it's warm, Grandad wears a bucket hat almost balanced on top of his head rather than pulling it down. From our vantage point in the ferns, you can mostly just see the disembodied hat floating along and is something we love to mock him for!

My Uncle is notorious for blowing out the candles on other people's birthday cakes when you're singing happy birthday to them. But when it's his own cake and birthday, he doesn't want to blow them out at all! Such a silly tradition but something we do every year and I always look forward to seeing how long he'll refuse to blow his own candles out!

## Monday 28th September

Thank goodness for starting to feeling better. I am entirely behind on all my planning and resources, but I don't think I would have made it if I hadn't stopped to rest on Saturday.

Dale came this morning grinning like a Cheshire cat. I asked him if there was something making him feel happy and this is what ensued...
Dale asked me "what do you do if your lunchbox is on the roof?"
I said, "well I'm not sure my lunchbox has ever been on the roof. Why would it be on the roof?"
Dale smiled a bit bigger and asked me again, "but what do you do if your lunchbox is on the roof?"
This child has gone mad, I thought. "Isn't that your lunchbox there, Dale?"
He jumped up and down a little bit here and repeated, "what do you do if your lunchbox is on the roof?"
At this point it dawned on me. He was trying to tell a joke and I hadn't realised, whoops, but that's technically on you, kid. His delivery was terrible, but he had only just turned four so perhaps I could forgive him, plus the punchline could still be gold. "OH! Ok, I don't know Dale, what do you do if your lunchbox is on the roof?"
"Get a ladder and go up and get it!"

Fail. Dale almost couldn't get through the sentence before he fell on the floor laughing his socks off. Bless him.

## Tuesday 29th September

I don't have kids so I don't know, but is it normal to put yourself to sleep whilst reading a bedtime story? Not that an end of the day story is meant to make them sleepy, it's slightly different, but Fabio put his hand up mid-The Gruffalo today and asked me why I always yawn when I'm reading them stories! I genuinely had no idea this was happening, but through the rest of the book I noticed I was yawning more and more! Though that I put down to him pointing it out and so the more I yawned the more I thought I needed to yawn. Interesting.

Bed time tonight was 9.15pm. It's getting earlier.

**Wednesday 30th September**

The whole class is now counting my yawns per story. I popped back over at the end of the day because the cover teacher had to leave early so I ended up reading them their end of the day story. Fabio recalled that it was five yawns yesterday and only three today. I'm pleased with his maths and his memory but I'm not sure I like the context. I haven't seen any of them yawn during story time...but then they are young and full of life, whereas I am always on the verge of napping.

**Thursday 1st October**

It's Slip into Slippers day tomorrow to raise money for old people. I am all in favour of this and am very excited for the comfiest day since Jeans for Genes day! Well done, charities. Well done.

In other, less charitable news, I had set up a space in the classroom for the curriculum area Understanding the World, where children could independently explore and create their own learning from resources out on shelves, including lots of science resources for investigations. Gosh did three boys investigate today. One resource in the investigation area was a selection of large, handheld tweezers for children to pick up leaves or blocks or whatever they wanted. Can you see where this is going? Three boys had sat themselves down next to each other, trousers and underwear around their ankles, each with a set of tweezers in their hand, trying to gently pinch their you-know-what's. The only saving grace was that at least they were only pinching their own genitals rather than each others'! That was a strange conversation to have with their parents.

Also, only one story-yawn today, or so I was informed.

**Friday 2nd October**

When I left for school this morning, I thought that what I'd be writing in my diary tonight would be something along the lines of - what a comfy day I've had! Now that it's come down to it, though, I'm not sure how I feel about it! It absolutely poured down all night so everything outside was soaking, meaning the children (and adults, I suppose) came in with really wet, dirty shoes. By the time they'd wandered over to the carpet to change into their slippers, the carpet was filthy! Perhaps it was lovely for those classes with older children who didn't have to be in their carpet space to change their shoes for risk of losing them immediately, but for us with the little's it was a nightmare! Plus, because they have free-flow access to the outside area at all times, the children were constantly changing their minds about where to be (their prerogative I guess) and so needed to change their shoes/slippers all the damn time! There were SO many shoes and slippers on the wrong feet!

Another problem, which you can probably guess, is walking into the toilets in slippers. Children can't aim. It's always gross in there, so then they're treading all of that around the classroom in lovely comfy slippers! Outrageous.

So now, my slippers are slightly dirty and covered in essence of children. They will very much become school slippers. I need new slippers. Apparently some settings have this as a standard, that children change into slippers whenever they're inside. I've gone off the idea.

**Saturday 3rd October**

I've realised that on Saturdays I tend to have really bad headaches and am really tired. The tiredness was pretty obviously down to the hectic work week so I'd just lumped the headaches in with that cause. But I think it's actually down to not drinking very much during the week. I'm finding that I'm guzzling squash throughout the day on a Saturday like I can't get enough, and it's occurred to me that I never really stop to give myself a drink break at work. Being in Reception we don't have break times other than stopped for snack, but I'm usually reading them a story. Then at lunch, I work through it to try to get admin done so that I can leave earlier after work before it's the middle of the night. So I might only have one or two drinks a day at work. I'm going to buy myself some sort of water bottle to carry round with me so that I can have more fluids and must stop being too busy to take care of myself.

**Sunday 4th October**

Went to my Grandparents' again today. I was eating a biscuit and my Grandad looked over at me and said "You'll never be a Slim Jim will you?" Cheers Grandad.

**Monday 5th October**

Flu nasal sprays. Not a particularly terrifying sounding event but we had some meltdowns today! They have a tiny squirt in their tiny noses and it's all done but they couldn't handle it. I wanted to yell at them that they know nothing of pain, just wait until they have to have a long needle shoved into the arm, but obviously their thresholds are slightly different from those of adults so I refrained. TTA bossed it, she was having none of their nonsense. I'm starting to really enjoy her. It still took up most of our day somehow. Some of them 'needed' a tissue constantly for the rest of the day. It was like a scene from Pride and Prejudice with delicate women needing handkerchiefs all the time.

(Bed time: 9pm. Send help)

**Tuesday 6th October**

I am quickly learning that teachers experience the whole range of emotions when working with children. Sometimes it breaks your heart, other times there's no space in your own feelings for the person who had to wait until next time to be at the front of the line. On occasion, I have definitely had to hold back from telling

them – you don't know what suffering is! But I have held back. I definitely don't want to shout that at a child at all, never mind when they're in turmoil. Once you get to the bottom of what's making a child feel that particular way, you can normally relate to them, empathise, share in the feeling with them, counsel them through it. There are, however, moments where you can't really empathise and won't quite know what to say, like this one from today:
"Oh Steve, what's the matter?"
(Sobbing) "Clive."
"Ok, tell me what happened."
(Wailing) "He said my dinosaur is smaller than his."

Steve was holding one of the smallest toy dinosaurs I'd ever seen. Not quite polly pocket size, but it easily fit into his four-year-old palm. I looked over at Clive who looked utterly bemused, holding a giant diplodocus that was almost as big as his entire head. I tried to be gentle...
"Well sweetheart, it is smaller than Clive's dinosaur..."
Here I expected him to howl that he wanted a bigger one or that Clive had taken it off him. No no...
"But I don't want him to SAY it!"
Seriously, what do you do with this?

I was very apologetic to his Mum at the end of the day that he had had such a traumatic experience and that I was only able to try to talk him through how to handle life's disappointments, but she just laughed and said "oh don't worry, he is just so sensitive." Good to know.

**Wednesday 7th October**

We are a month into the school year and Rahul still cannot pronounce my name. He is this wonderful, tiny person who was born premature so is so much smaller than anyone else, English is his second language and his voice comes out all high-pitched. 'Miss Youngwood' is just too much for him at the moment, so whenever he needs me he simply squeaks "YOUNG!" across the classroom at me. It makes me smile every time.

**Thursday 8th October**

I've been looking ahead for Phonics and trying to diversify how we're teaching it. I've been thinking about Letterland, which is how I learned letters at school. There was Dippy Duck (be careful saying that one fast), Munching Mike, Kicking King. Letters were given characters and through a story, children learned the sounds of the alphabet. Most people who aren't teachers or parents don't know what Phonics is... let's face it, some parents don't even have a clue, because that's like knowing what medulloblastoma means when you're not a medical professional (I just looked it up, it sounds awful, I've obviously watched too much Grey's Anatomy). I didn't know what Phonics was when I started teacher training, but I sure do remember Letterland being up in the classroom when I was a kid. I also remember being genuinely disappointed that the story about the starting letter of my name was male 'Firefighter Fred', but at least it wasn't boring like Lucy Lamp Light. I hope these children get something from my Phonics lessons, it's taking so much of me to make them interesting and keep it interesting. The pace of it is incredible and some children are already struggling to keep up but I'm determined to not leave anyone behind.

**Friday 9th October**

"Give me a word that rhymes with fit... "
"Shit!"
This accurately summarises my day.

**Saturday 10th October**

What a day! Flu jab, doctor's appointment to get my repeat prescription, hairdresser and car service. This is a week's worth of activities, why on earth have I crammed them into one day? Oh, because by the time I finish work on a weekday everything is closed.

**Sunday 11th October**

I met up with a friend this morning who is currently doing a PGCE in primary education. She's just started her first placement and is absolutely loving it! You know those people who just seem to fit with their job? I can absolutely see that she'd be excellent with children. She's fun and silly and always seems to be able to find joy in things, even when she's tired or a bit down. I'd love to see her teach. She's still managing to live the uni life though, partying and what not. I cannot go out in the week anymore. I'm drained of most of my energy by Tuesday afternoon so I don't know how she does it. She's also more sociable than me though, and always was. I often felt like I was a tag-along in our friendship group, never quite fitting in, or maybe I did but just didn't believe it. I find people quite draining. Mum and Di always seem to be with other people and can't seem to get enough, but I need time to just be. Especially considering all day every day at work is talking and playing and having to be so excited about everything! I can't do it all weekend too.

**Monday 12th October**

Today was adorable! It was school photograph day where the children have individual photos taken and then ones with their siblings. It was mild chaos with children going in and out, but then working in the early years is pretty chaotic anyway. I was chatting with a teacher from Year 3 who was struggling to know how to get anything done. They start with the little ones because they're more likely to end up caked in mud or snot or whatever else by lunchtime, so it means that the higher up the school you are the more you just sort of wait around to be called. Then you have to make sure everyone has their jumper on with the collar out, there are no pen marks on anyone's faces and entertain them while you wait for each individual to have their photograph taken. Then, individuals are called out to go have photos with their siblings, so I feel really bad for the teachers in the older year groups because it doesn't exactly provide a calm learning environment!

Bernard just would not get in front of the camera. Like, at all. There's being shy and then there's mild terror. Poor kid. Everyone else had gone back to the classroom with TTA, and I spent a good ten minutes trying to coerce this child into standing in front of the camera by persuading him that I'd be in it with him!! Surprise, Bernard's parents, it's a school photo of your son and his teacher! I gradually edged out until our fingers were just touching. Hopefully they got something to send home to his parents. I wonder what that's about. He doesn't have the best grasp of English and doesn't really speak much, so it's difficult to know. But we got something at least.

**Tuesday 13th October**

Parents evening number one. Too tired. 13-hour day including a vomiter and a biter (kids, not parents). Too tired.

**Wednesday 14th October**

Parents evening number two. Who on earth decided that you should work a full day, then do four hours of back-to-back meetings? Twice in one week! Too tired. Details tomorrow.

(Bed time: 8.45pm)

**Thursday 15th October**

Parent. Evenings. Suck. They suck. Like, really suck. I barely had any voice left for my actual teaching today and the children still had their usual amount of energy so I don't quite understand the science of teaching after two days of parents' evenings.

If you take away my exhausted grumpiness, it was actually quite nice to do parents evening. It's so manic on the door each morning and afternoon that I haven't got to know everyone properly. There are some absolute cracking parents in the class! Humorous parents, honest parents, supportive parents, engaging parents, generous parents, whacky parents (my personal favourites) and the just generally friendly parents. So many of them asked genuine questions about their child and lots of them weren't about how many words they could now read compared to September, but how happy they were in school and whether or not they were kind to other children. My heart almost exploded when one parent asked me that last one. Frances' Dad wasn't overly happy that she had cut her own hair, but he also understood that we can't have our eyes on every single child every single second of the day. As someone who does not have children of her own, I am in absolute awe of these wonderful parents who battle through their own lives, whilst keeping another human being alive, happy and well. They're superhuman.

Then there are the bellends.

Occasionally people feel very stressed or angry or upset about something and it all gets fired at you as the teacher. Fine. Sometimes, you'll make a mistake (being a human and all). Fine. But there are some parents who seem like they've made it their mission in life to be a pain in your behind, and sitting down face-to-face, remaining composed and professional with those parents was hard work. I shall remember these morons. You want to come on our next class trip? Ok I'll add your name... oh no your name didn't come out of the hat. It appeared to fold itself four times more than the other names so it was too small to grasp, what a shame. You want to reserve a seat for the Christmas production? Oh I'm so sorry it's standing room only now, good luck to you. You booked this parents' evening slot? Gosh darn it the system appears to have double booked so you'll have to wait for half an hour, oh what an absolute catastrophe. Suck it.

Teachers are superheroes, in my honest opinion, but we do not actually have real magical powers. I'm sorry that Phyllis had a paper cut and that it was left untreated, but she didn't actually tell us about it – there's not a lot of scope for me to notice the tiniest scratch in the world and that can't be my fault! Perhaps Stuart did bring home a reading book for the second time, is it the end of the world? Have you never read the same book twice? Get a grip!

At least there are a few months to go before the next round. I've had enough of people.

**Friday 16th October**

I like to think of myself as, at the very least, not boring. I believe I'm taking so well to teaching because I am a little bit nuts at heart, and working with children, especially four and five-year-olds, is allowing me to be just that. A little bit nuts. No four-year-old wants a strict teacher; yes, there are boundaries that must be put in place, we can't have javelins being thrown around willy nilly, but they need fun and joy and ridiculousness. However, not all of the children in my class necessarily 'get me' and they can be very, very, very honest, or very uncomprehending. It also works the other way, in that I just don't understand some of these children! I do, however, know that they are just as ridiculous and silly as me, which is a delight. Dashes is a girl from Turkey with a beginning grasp on English; she barely spoke at all through September but she came running over and told me this joke today:

*Knock knock...*
Who's there?
*Dasha...*
Dasha who?
*Dasha orange!!*

She then fell about laughing her head off and I had to just smile along with her. Is it just me? Do you get it? She's been telling me this joke day after day after day, which is lovely because it obviously means that her grasp of English and her confidence are developing. But I would've liked her to take some constructive criticism on her content.

**Sunday 18th October**

Di and I are up at Dad's for the weekend. He lives in Cumbria so it's a lovely four hour journey after work on a Friday night! It's a beautiful place though, right up in the mountains right next to a farmer and his field, and always great to see Dad. I love the countryside, always have. Dad used to take us walking in the Lake District a lot and we sure have climbed some mountains in our time!

I'm not even sure what his job is up there; he claims he's "running Cumbria". He's not, but you know what? He probably could. Dad didn't grow up with a lot, there were ten of them in a two-bed house, but Nan and Grandad had an amazing work ethic and this passed down to him. He didn't do brilliantly at school (unless you count the different ways he managed to torture his teachers!) but still managed to work his way up to be really successful and I've always admired him for that. I genuinely don't think there's anything he doesn't know, but part of that is his amazing ability to bullshit about the stuff he isn't sure of so you think he knows it all anyway!

**Sunday 18th October**

A weekend is never quite long enough to visit someone you don't see very often. We don't arrive until about 9pm Friday night and then we leave after lunch on the Sunday. It's hard work after working such a long week and then starting to think about Monday morning and what's going to come at me when the children arrive. Weekends are still lovely at the moment but I'm starting to notice being more tired and needing to do a bit more work to finish off a week or prepare for the next one.

**Monday 19th October**

Ok. It's official. I hate scarecrows. They're meant to scare crows, yet here I am, a human being, terrified of inanimate objects! As part of our harvest festival we held a scarecrow competition and all the entries had to come in today. Wow. Just wow. There were some incredible efforts! Lifesize, minion based, pumpkin themed, you name it there was a scarecrow to represent it. One parent said they'd been to a pet store and bought an insane amount (my words, not hers) of hay to stuff their scarecrow with! That is commitment! I wonder what they'll do with them when we send them back home. I hope they know they're taking them back home! It's not too long until Bonfire Night, I wonder if they'll use them as Guys and chuck them on a garden bonfire. I wouldn't be keeping any of them in the lounge, that's for sure! There are some creepy things sitting in that hall. Maybe it's so much worse because there are so many of them. The fact that the hall lights are on motion sensors doesn't help. Walking into a dark hall filled with creepers is literally like walking into a horror movie.

**<u>Tuesday 20th October</u>**

I stood on a table today to hang something from the ceiling when I wobbled and nearly fell off the table. I looked round and there was five-year-old Betty, stood next to me with surprised, wide eyes like I'd nearly fallen and crushed her. In my embarrassment, I said "now that's why you don't stand on tables" – as if she had been the one clambering around without the safety of an actual ladder! Poor child.

**<u>Wednesday 21st October</u>**

So, it's officially freezing in school. Not literally, but officially. I have two things to say about this:

1. The site manager is refusing to turn the heating on until after half term. I am livid. Why don't we just turn it on when we're all icicles rather than when a certain date comes around?
2. The children either do not feel the cold or they really feel the cold. Half of the class are legging it around outside in just their t-shirts and we're having to work really hard at

> getting them to wear and zip up their coats. Savages. The other half of the class are standing about moaning that it's cold, with balaclavas and mittens, dressed up like eskimos, refusing to move around to warm themselves up.

We're in for a long term, folks.

(Bed time: still 8.45pm)

**Thursday 22nd October**

Today was hard work. I mean, it's always hard work in one way or another, but this morning I could've just walked outside and cried. I could not get a single four or five-year-old to tell me what we learned yesterday. I looked imploring at the sea of blank, expectant faces staring back at me. "Anybody?" Nothing. "Hello?" Nothing. I closed my eyes for a second and took a deep breath in. Two more get ups, I remember thinking, as if measuring your remaining working days before a holiday in 'get ups' was acceptable as an adult.

"Ok. Let's try this a different way," I said, opening my eyes and forcing a smile through my tired face. I wasn't just tired, I was exhausted. Mr Phillips had asked me if I'd had a late-night last night. "Nope, in bed at nine...but thanks for that, boss" I had replied. How rude! Not a great move. Still, at least I'd managed to apply mascara to both eyes this morning as opposed to last week when I was half a glamourous, elegant supermodel (to quote Eddie Izzard – in my mind) and half a makeup-less zombie. I got some really strange looks that day.

Anyway I can't blame those tiny humans for forgetting my outstanding teaching. Every Monday when my year partner asks me how my weekend was, I have to pause and think for a while to remember what I'd done. "Uh fine...I think?!" was my usual stock answer before I'd properly woken up. A quick aside here, I realise I have mentioned being tired a number of times already...settle in because that's basically the theme of my life. This diary should've been called "I'm Tired". Isn't being an adult just telling other adults how tired you are for no reason then waiting to hear why they're so tired? You know the ones. It's Monday, they have a young child, it's Tuesday, they have teenagers, it's Wednesday, you worked late, you were out partying hard...HA! The Early Years Foundation Stage leader said you won't hear that last one unless it's the morning after the Christmas party and everyone is cursing the fools that decided Thursday was a much better day for a knees up than Friday. (She also told me that this is always fine, I should whack a film on and use the time to take down my Christmas displays. Apparently when you've made it through the Nativity production, the children's Christmas party and end of term assessments, you can just relax. I've heard a few members of staff saying that Netflix is a wonderful teacher. I'm not so sure.)

So, there I was, sat looking at thirty wonderful but vacant faces, scratch that – twenty faces, five backs of heads, a couple of bums in the air and some empty spaces for those who were off or in the toilet, and I dug down deep for that hope, optimism and excitement that I felt on my first, first day.

"Ok, let's try this a different way. Who can remember the very special guest we had in yesterday? Yes, Johnathan?"

It's happened! Someone has remembered yesterday's lesson! Thank goodness. I don't speak French past random food items or to ask where the swimming pool is, but sometimes I wondered if I had accidentally started speaking fluent French to them by some absolutely incredible miracle. But no, here was Johnathan to save the day! Thank goodness for Johnathan.

"I like sausages," says Johnathan. Right. Well. Not quite what I had in mind but hey, the ball was rolling, we had participation and this was glorious. I had to hand it to Johnathan, he'd got four other children to put their hands up, so regardless of the absurdity of his answer we were in business! Here we go, well done Johnathan, my trusty sidekick, you might have been completely off piste but let's see what they remember...

"I like sausages too!" says Katerina.
"I had sausages for breakfast!" pipes up Claudio.
"I have sausages all the time, for every meal!" Jim lies. I know it is a lie because Jim has packed lunches and I've never seen a sausage in there. I didn't point this out in front of the whole class, though.

Well, thanks a lot Johnathan. You derailed my already sticky lesson introduction. This shall be reflected in your report, I thought to myself with a mental image of me 'hehehe-ing' and tapping my fingers together like Mr Burns, with a mixture of glee and realism that this was absolutely not something to go in a child's report. *Johnathan thinks about sausages too much.* Or maybe *Johnathan struggles to stay on task because he loves sausages.* That's a bit harsh based on one comment but it was a possibility if he didn't sort himself out.

"Wow ok, that's fantastic sausage news, thank you everyone for your input! Feel free to tell your friends at break time what your favourite food is, put it in a spreadsheet and then show me the PowerPoint tomorrow morning," I teased. A few of them laughed. Some of them got me. Mostly they probably thought I was an idiot. I fall over a lot and drop things all the time.

I looked over at TTA who was grinning at me, in a way that said "you're on your own but I'll be over here enjoying it all".

**<u>Friday 23rd October</u>**

We had a new kid start today; Blake. I'm not sure about this one. He had a hard time coming in at the beginning, which is totally understandable because we're half a term in, on the last day before a holiday and everyone already knows each other. New schools are hard, especially in the middle of an academic year. So TTA and I both worked hard to make him feel at home. He settled in ok but when things didn't go his way he started to have a little tantrum. When he was doing a jigsaw, Fabio went over to join in and Blake just shoved him over. When he found out that apples were the snack, he refused to have one. Then later he wanted a snack but they'd been put back in the kitchen in the other building so he pushed over the lunchbox trolly. I know it's his first day and life is hard, but I'm a bit nervous about his reactions to things. At the end of the day his Dad said he'd never seen anything like that from him before, so perhaps he was just struggling with the change.

A good time for a holiday I think! I've got to come in for a couple of days though to catch up with uploading their photos and observations to their learning journeys and change some displays. Not exactly a week's holiday but still nice to have some time to rest.

**Saturday 24th October**

I was building up to asking a guy on a date who I've been chatting to online. But I'm not sure I like his banter. We were chatting about who could 'teach whom a lesson', and in response to me saying "Oh please, you'd get your ass handed to you", he said "Yeah well I would smash your head into a curb"... I decided to call it quits right about then. That doesn't seem too funny to me.

**Sunday 25th October**

One of our favourite Birmingham rock clubs is closing soon; Subway City. It's so much fun and just another rock club to be closing down, I wonder if there will be any left! I'm going to go with a mate and a load of his mates, who incidentally are all people I know through school or my sister so that'll be fun. I'm really gutted that it's closing but at the same time I can't remember the last time I went...

I've done so little this weekend. I'm starting to notice how tired I am at the weekends and am less and less able or inclined to see people or do things. At least I have a week so there's a bit more time to see people or do things, but I'm just getting more and more exhausted. I'm still going to bed about 9pm, even at the weekends. Lame.

**Wednesday 28th October**

How, HOW have I spent two days of my holiday in school?! This is madness. People always talk about teachers having all this holiday, but I have had so much to do. I did leave about 4pm on Friday but even if I had stayed until 6pm I would still have basically done two days. Mum came in with me yesterday as she had a day off for building up some toil. Funny that, how teachers tend to work double their weekly hours, yet the holiday we get isn't seen as collecting overtime or having a well-deserved rest. Anyway, I'm going to do FUN things for the rest of the week to make up for losing two days to work. And by fun, I mostly mean activities I can do in my PJs, which is what today has consisted of. TV and the sofa. It really upset my Dad who thinks there's more to life than TV. Perhaps there is, but for one day it has not hurt me one little bit.

**Thursday 29th October**

West Midlands Safari Park is the absolute bomb (urgh I'm not cool enough to pull that saying off). I went with a couple of friends and we had such a blast! The elephants are the best bit for me. I refused to feed any animals but have a brilliant video of one friend getting the entire right side of her body licked by a giraffe! I remember coming here with friends when I was about 17 and people were just starting to get their driving licences and a couple got their own cars. Trouble is, when you're 17 you tend to get a really really old, really really rubbish car. The one I was passenger in was thankfully find one, but we kept seeing the other car in our party steaming! It was a very different experience today inn a half decent car with much less fear about what the monkeys might destroy!

(Bed time: I pushed it to 10.30pm tonight!!!!!)

**Friday 30th October**

How is it not even the next month and I'm out of money? I shopped hard today, I'm really good at it. Spending money, acquiring new clothes and tat; these could go under special skills on my cv. I'm also doing lots of house shopping even though I currently don't have a house to be shopping for! My poor Mum now has boxes and boxes of cutlery and plates and bedding and artificial flowers and all sorts in the spare room. She keeps warning me that I might get into a house and change my mind or the stuff I've bought won't fit the style, but I can't help it. I've got all my colour schemes planned out (red in the lounge, purple in the bedroom, pink in the bathroom, green in the kitchen, a pale turquoise-style blue in the spare room, if I have one) and I can't seem to stop myself from buying pretty things to fill all the surfaces I don't yet have. I haven't bought anything big like a sofa so I don't know what Mum's moaning about, there's loads of space. I might, however, need to set up some sort of budgeting scheme for myself so that when we get paid on 24th of a month, I'm not in my overdraft within a week.

**Saturday 31st October**

I hate Halloween. I really hate it. We're teaching children to blackmail strangers, has anyone else realised this? I was home alone tonight and dreading it. I had two groups of young children ring the doorbell and I had to smile and tell them how scary they are whilst giving them sweets. Most of them had put no effort in at all and had just put on a shop-bought outfit. Some of them weren't even scary! There was a fairy and a ladybird! It's not just fancy dress, come on now.

The worst was when I opened the door to three teenagers, who were wearing sweats (like me) but had just put a cheap Scary Movie mask on. They stood there in silence and jingled their pockets at me. Are you SERIOUS? You want paying for turning up at my door in the worst costume ever? See...blackmail. I smiled as I handed them a Werther's Original each and then locked the door behind them. I'm surprised we don't have eggs all over the house.

**Sunday 1st November**

How is it November already? I am not emotionally prepared for it to be Monday again tomorrow. I'm not sure where this week or this month have gone.

# Chapter 2
# Autumn term 2

**Monday 2nd November**
I got asked by little Frasier why my jumper had a label on the outside of it today. At about 11am. A good four hours into the day for me. Christ.

I felt like saying, it shouldn't be there, kid. The jumper is inside out. The polite thing to do, is to quietly whisper in someone's ear "I thought you'd like to know that your jumper is inside out and has been all morning" but no, fine, just announce it really loudly and point so that everyone can see.

It wasn't the child's fault. They should be asking questions. We encourage this. It's the whole point of being a teacher; to nourish the minds of the young in our care. But I'm tired and in shock after getting up.ao early for the first time in a week and that sucked. What was worse, was when I took off the jumper to turn it the right way, I discovered that the reason I'd felt like I was choking all morning was that my t-shirt was back to front.

What the hell, Monday?

**Tuesday 3rd November**
Today was weird. The headteacher introduced Operation Christmas Child, where people can buy toys or healthcare products and put them in a decorated shoebox to send to children around the world. It was such an passionate speech about children who don't have their own toys, don't get Christmas presents, some don't even have a toothbrush. I came out of that assembly feeling so humbled and grateful for my life.

We got back to the classroom and Jiminy started crying his eyes out. So I figured, poor little mite, he's feeling so bad for these children that he can't handle it. So I went over to give him some comfort and he balled "I don't want to give away any of my toys!" Wow. I told him that the point isn't to get rid of your stuff, it's to buy things for children who have nothing of their own, not even shoes sometimes, and he just cried harder and was adamant that he was not going to give anything of his away. I just had no idea what to do with this! I was incensed on behalf of those children that aren't as lucky as Jiminy, but then also checked myself. This kid is only 4. He obviously has some selflessness to learn. I made a mental note to work on this. Good Lord.

**Wednesday 4th November**

Blake is genuinely concerning me. He's had a good couple of days, came in happily and everything, but really wants to have things his own way. Refuses to sit on the carpet with everyone else, gets a bit bolshy if we ask him to do anything. I got called in today from my non-contact time to help out when he started getting cross and yelling at everyone. I've spoken to his Dad again about it potentially being a tricky transition time but he said Blake is happy and settled and is already talking about how much he loves it here. These two pictures of this child do not add up.

In other news, ahead of Remembrance Day, the school are selling poppies. And bracelets. And keyrings, and slap bands and badges and every other annoying thing that gets lost the INSTANT a child pays for it. We're having to keep track of all of their money and help them buy things, only to insist they stay in their bookbags because they just immediately go walkabout and they're all accusing each other of theft. It's amazing how quickly they can turn on their best mate if the fate of a slap band is at stake. This is going to be every day this week.

Send help.

**Thursday 5th November**

Blake slapped me in the face today. He had spat in someone's face who was trying to play in the sand with him, so I bent down to talk to him about what he was feeling and he slapped me in the face and walked off. What the actual hell? We managed to have a conversation about it and again I talked to his Dad, who again seemed really shocked, but in a shifty kind of way that makes me think this isn't actually a surprise. It was interesting seeing him trying to talk to Blake, who started shouting and walking off and it felt like the Dad had no idea what to do, but then it's tough to parent an angry child when people are watching so I suggested they go home and talk about it when he had calmed down.

I went and checked his records after school and it turns out that he was asked to leave his last Nursery because of his violent behaviour! Apparently they have this whole paper trail of incidents that had happened with no support from parents until they finally had to ask him to leave because it was out of control, and they had kept him at home from then until he had to start school. No wonder it felt like the Dad's account didn't match up to what we were seeing with Blake at school, they're obviously in utter denial or they didn't want us to know! This is one for the deputy head / behaviour lead I think.

**Friday 6th November**

I've got so much work to do this weekend, I don't know where it keeps coming from after working between nine and twelve hours a day. I was sat at my desk finishing some planning at about 6pm and I kid you not, a cat wandered in and jumped up into my lap!! Maybe I am starting to live here if the wildlife are flocking to me. a sign to go home.

**Saturday 7th November**

And just like that, Subway City is no more. We went last night and it was amazing! A mate from school invited me and I went round to his house first. He shares it with a bunch of other guys and turns out, I know a load of them! There's a couple of guys who I've known since I was about 2 because our Mums are friends from playgroup, a guy I know through them, a couple of guys who were mates with my sister in school (and I didn't have the best time in the early years so I spent a lot of time hanging out with them). I spent a lot of time in this guy ' room as he's got a huge sofa and everyone was congregated in there. It was a really good night, the place was really busy and they played all the best songs from the last few years, though a few of them preferred the heavy metal room whereas I was upstairs with the punks and emos! I am absolutely hanging today, though. Mum tried to enlist me into helping the garden again; we've got a couple of really big trees at the back that drop all of their leaves in our garden so it takes a lot of raking. I helped a bit but was mostly the child jumping in the piles, which wasn't very helpful.

The best thing about today though is that we went to a Bonfire night celebration at our local park. It was awesome! Bonfire Night is my favourite night of the year. There are crunchy leaves on the ground, you get the smell of wood smoke in the cold air, you get to look like an idiot trying to eat a toffee apple, and then there are all the fireworks! It's just magical and I love it. I was too tired to do owt on Thursday for actual Bonfire Night but tonight was great. We even took our own sparklers, though they don't have the same effect now as I remember them having when I was a kid. After about ten seconds it's like ok, that's done, now what? Still, an all time great evening.

**Sunday 8th November**

Bonfire smoke is gorgeous when you're in it, but the next morning it's disgusting!

We went over to my grandparents' again today. We normally have a roast for lunch and then something lighter in the evening and today we requested a raclette! It always fills them with such dread but Di and I have always loved it. I only found out recently that raclette is actually a cheese, and what we've been talking about our whole lives is an indoor grill thing that is for the cheese, but we've never actually had raclette cheese! There are 8 little pans that go round under a grill that you can put cheese or tomato or mushrooms etc. in, and then a whole plate on top to put other stuff. It's so quiet to begin with while it warms up and you wait for the first round, then you end up manically waving a pan of cheese in someone's face yelling "do you need cheese? I already have so much, who needs this damn cheese!" It's hilarious and wonderful and I just love it. I've had a bit of a scratchy throat today but I'm guessing that's just the leftover hangover from Friday night!

**Monday 9th November**

It's not leftover hangover. I'm ill. Again. You have got to be kidding me. I had to call in sick, I woke up with huge glands and a high temperature. I feel utterly miserable and I mostly hate that someone else is in my classroom teaching my children. I hadn't realised how controlling I am until today! The classroom was set up and ready to go, thank goodness for being organised, and TTA will kick ass as usual, so everything is ready and won't fall apart, but I hate that I'm not there.

(Bed time: all throughout the day)

**Tuesday 10th November**

The guilt of having two days off is incredible. I almost feel like I don't deserve to be off sick because we get so many holidays. But there's no way I could work through this, it's so much worse than my first round of teacher illness. The trouble is, I'm still doing my planning because I don't want to fall behind with it. I know I won't get better properly if I'm not resting but I can't not do it, it takes so long and I don't want to be unprepared. This sucks.

**Wednesday 11th November**

I went back in this morning, mostly because I figured after I saw the parents and children on their way in, I'd pop off to the staff room for my non-contact day and be able to work at my own pace, quietly without having to talk to too many people.. Everyone was so lovely, the children had really missed me and a couple of parents asked how I was feeling. Apart from Donald's Mum, who made a beeline for me straight away to have a go at me for sending home reading books that are below his ability. I tried to explain that it's not just about reading the words it's also about comprehension and that he wasn't very able to talk about the pictures or the story or the characters yet, and she just got really cross and demanded he be moved up a level. I should have had another day off, my throat can't cope with this level of rudeness or stupidity.

Also, trying to do a minute's silence with four and five year olds is insane. I popped back in to be with them for it and they did really well, bless them, but children are not meant to be quiet!

**Thursday 12th November**

Blake threw a chair at me today. Because I asked him to pick up a pencil he'd dropped. Is it pathetic to be developing a fear of this child? He can be so happy and lovely and then he'll chuck furniture at me for a really simple request. I'm still not feeling great and this on top of that just sucks. I've asked for the behaviour lead to come and do an assessment or observation on him. I don't really know what to do with this.

(Bed time: 8.30pm)

**Friday 13th November**

Children in need! We had such a fun day, aside from the fact that once again the children were in their own clothes and this makes them mental. So many of them were wearing Pudsey ears which is just one of the cutest things I've ever seen, but I ended up with a pile of Pudsey ears on my desk by approximately 9.06am. We had quite a few tears today, I think their emotions were just through the roof with all the excitement and difference in routine. We joined the whole school assembly but TTA spent the whole of it in the corridors with Blake who absolutely refused to come in and walked up and down the corridors slamming doors. We've started a behaviour log and it's already spanning a few pages. The deputy (also behaviour lead) had come to assess him this morning and of course he had been golden, but luckily she saw this display so has got an idea of what's going on. She suggested a visual timetable, a box of things he likes to distract him when he's triggered and perhaps a bean bag or tent for him to 'hide' in. I think we all need our own tents to hide in.

I am so happy it's Friday.

**Saturday 14th November**

Bed all day. I'm feeling a bit better but still not 100%.

**Sunday 15th November**

An interesting turn of events; that guy Eddie from the Subway City night added me on Facebook. I'd accepted and he started a chat with me, right when I was making a risotto. The thing with risotto is you have keep stirring it and keep adding the liquid little by little. I'm pretty good at it and didn't think much of it. Also didn't think too much of chatting with Eddie. We barely talked to each other that night we all went out, he was absolutely hammered and I mostly stuck with the guys I already knew. But today? We were two hours into chatting on messenger and I realised that the risotto was ruined from me not paying the slightest bit of attention to it.

I can come across as quite confident. My parents always encouraged me to be polite and friendly and talk to people, but I've never found it easy. I mentioned before about never feeling like I properly fit in anywhere and so I always assume people won't like me so what's the point? But with Eddie...it was so easy. We barely even talked about generic conversation stuff (what you do for work, where did you grow up, how many siblings do you have etc.); we just talked nonsense! I found myself with a stupid sickly smile on my face after we were done talking.

**Monday 16th November**

I'm still not back to feeling 'normal', whatever that is for me, but feel like I'm at a stage where I can cope with working. This is great news, because it is anti-bullying week.

Have you ever tried to introduce a new concept to children? They had no idea what it was before but suddenly, that concept is everywhere. Well, that's exactly what happens when you talk about bullying.

"She sneezed at me, she's bullying me!"
"I'm being bullied, he fell over and when he fell over he kicked me."
"They're bullying each other, they're both hiding from each other."

Ok, everyone back to the carpet, let's talk about bullying again!

**Tuesday 17th November**

I invited Gary's parents in for a meeting after school today because I'm really worried about his progress. He's a lovely little boy who's always dressing up and pretending, he's happy and polite and so funny. But his motor skills are really poor. He walks like he's floating on a cloud, has very little strength in his hands so things like putting his coat on is really tricky for him, and he can barely hold a pencil. Since the first week, we've been getting the children to practise writing their names every day. If they have no idea, they have their name to trace over, if they have some idea they can trace it then practise it underneath, and if they move past that they can then just copy it or write it from memory. At this point, some still can't use a tripod grip on their pencil but every single one of them can trace over some shapes. Except Gary. Gary holds a pencil like it's too much hard work, barely makes any marks on the paper because he can't press down hard enough and cannot follow the patterns of his name. I've tried giving him simple lines and circles but still no. Hence the meeting.

His mum ripped me apart! I went in softly and said that we'd need to work on this moving forwards and she started demanding to see evidence of his poor skills and evidence of all the interventions we've been putting in place to date. It turns out that she is also a Reception teacher, but hasn't wanted to push him academically at home just because she's a teacher. She wants him to follow his own dreams. I love this and think it's admirable, but at some point when you're teaching a whole class of children that are the same age as your son, do you not realise that you need to put SOME effort into his physical strength because he is so far behind the others?! I'm hoping I managed to repair the relationship before she left but she seemed really cross and her husband didn't say a word the entire time! I wonder if it's guilt or if she just took it personally because I was telling her about a concern about her only child, but I was expecting a much more reasonable conversation!

**Wednesday 18th November**

Johnathan has been telling me for a week that there's a green lizard in his toilet. He's super imaginative and is always walking around holding a minimum of one plastic animal, normally an octopus, so I figured he was just being cute and creative. He's asked me a couple of times if there's a green lizard in my toilet and I keep telling him that lizards generally don't hang out in toilets. I discussed this with his Mum today. Turns out, it's one of those gel discs you put in for freshness. Bless him.

(Bed time: 9.45pm, what the hell?!)

**Thursday 19th November**

I've discovered that I both adore the office staff and am completely terrified of them! There are two wonderful ladies working within the office and they... Know... Everything. Literally everything! I feel so bad for them because I think I'm in there or emailing them every day with questions as I'm still new and learning the ropes, but gosh there isn't anything they haven't known! I hope I'm like that one day, though I don't seem to have a great memory. I can remember things like how many skittles were in a doubly filled packet once but not anything important, like my bank card pin code. They're so great when they're terrifying when it's directed at other people! I've had a couple of issues with parents and they've taken them over and they, in the nicest possible way, reminded me of dragons protecting a castle! So professional but you wouldn't cross them.

I think I'm in love with them.

**Friday 20th November**

Me: "give me a word that rhymes with snap..."
Dale: "crap!"
He's not wrong.

**Saturday 21st November**

I've been so busy all week that I haven't thought too much about Eddie, but we were chatting back and forth a bit and have exchanged numbers. He suggested I download WhatsApp, which is like messenger on your phone, so I did that and we have spent the entire day chatting nonsense. I definitely like this guy.

**Sunday 22nd November**

Mum and I went to look at some more houses today; a few more maisonettes but then some actual (albeit tiny) houses! There were some I was moderately excited by, but I don't think I've found 'the one' yet.

In other news, I've realised that I'm getting really lazy with indicating when I'm driving. I got most of the way home from the maisonettes and houses until I was turning right and saw a pigeon on the path. I put my indicator on. I'm now indicating for pigeons. Not people or cars. Just pigeons.

I'm losing it.

**Monday 23rd November**

I heard a parent promise to buy their kid a new doll if they went up a reading level. What is it with the pushy parents in this class? Why can't they just enjoy reading stories together? We read with them three times a week and as soon as they're not being challenged any more they will get more difficult books, but I keep trying to explain to parents that it's not about the complexity of the words, it's about their enjoyment, their comprehension, experiencing different genres and developing opinions. I genuinely think they switch off when I'm telling them these things and just immediately revert back to "ok but how can I get them to move up a level?" I can hear them swapping levels in the playground. This is insane!

**Tuesday 24th November**

Now I don't know about anyone else, but when I see a child who

has finished drinking from a cup and is sucking it to their face without using their hands, I say "Whoa look at you, you've got a cup for a mouth... You're now a cup-mouth!" I don't even know how else a person would respond to such an event? This happened this morning with Isadora, and she found this absolutely hysterical (and why wouldn't she, I'm a delight). Every time she had a drink of water from a cup, she would make it cling to her face and come and stare at me until I said something like "Oh look, it's cup-mouth!" Isadora came up to me later on in the afternoon and sat down next to me. She looked a bit sad so I said, "Hey, Isadora, have you got a joke for me?" She thought for a minute and then smiled. She said "Miss Youngwood, I've got a joke for you," (like it was her idea). She then leaned in really close and said "do you remember cup-mouth?" I smiled and said I remembered, and she burst out laughing. I waited for a little while before realising that that was the whole joke! So I laughed along, bless her. For the rest of the afternoon, every so often, Isadora would just sidle up to me, casual as could be, and murmur in my ear "...cup-mouth!" and oh how we laughed! One of us more heartily than the other if I'm honest.

**Wednesday 25th November**

Despite the fact that there are no pillows, duvets or beds of any sort in the classroom, Donald is convinced I live at school. I mentioned something about home and he was so confused. We had a chat about me not living in the classroom but he's not having any of it. When I pointed out that he comes to school every day but he doesn't live there, he just replied that I'm always there before and after him and he never sees me leave! I am here a lot. Sometimes it does feel like I live here. It's so funny that the children think I live here, but adults think I only work 9-3, when actually the 10-12 hour days plus the weekends spent planning and resourcing are all encompassing.

**Thursday 26th November**

I thought I'd lost a kid today. This might have been the worst moment of my life. It was home time, and when his Mum came to the door I couldn't see him. I checked all around the classroom and the toilets and I couldn't find him anywhere. I called his name and nothing. I could've sworn I hadn't seen him leave the classroom but he wasn't there. We all went into panic mode and sprinted around the school and playground looking for him, calling his name. The little git was hiding (really well) in the toilets behind an open stall door. I've never been more scared. I don't know how he would've got out of the door without me seeing him but still. The realisation of the extent of my responsibilities over these children's safety is terrifying. Wine time.

**Friday 27th November**

It's still pretty early to be thinking about it but I've chosen the Christmas production. It's really short and simple and the songs are absolutely gorgeous! I'm so excited! We had a chat about it this morning and the children volunteered for certain parts and then we had to make some executive decisions, like not giving the kid that never speaks a main talking role!! I also had some fun allocating some of the less desirable roles. Yep, you're the donkey, Gerald, are you feeling good about kicking me last week? Oh you're cross that I won't let you lick the wooden dolls, Frasier...boom, you're a turkey. I jest of course, it's all based on who offers to do speaking parts and who wants to melt into the background and silently mouth the words to We Wish You a Merry Christmas. Mostly.

We started practising the songs and I feel SO Christmassy! I cannot wait for next week, we'll decorate the school and make the classroom Santa's Grotto and then I get to live my best life for a month.

**Saturday 28th November**

I don't want to be the person who's moaning about being tired all the time but I'm so tired! I did so little today. Except for meeting my sister's new boyfriend, Maximus. It didn't go great... he'd made her brownies (I already like him) and had put the offcuts in a bowl, so I thought hey I'll help out because nobody likes the offcuts. Turns out, he'd specifically set them aside for Di. Whoops! They've been messaging back and forth for a while and I always know when she's texting him because she gets this sappy little grin on her face. He's silly and fun and I think I like him for her!

**Sunday 29th November**

It's Di's birthday tomorrow so we all got together today to celebrate her; my grandparents and uncle too, of course. She's one of my all-time favourite people so I love her birthday. Mum and I put loads of happy birthday banners and signs up everywhere and Gran and Grandad made their insanely good fatless sponge cake. They always make it and then Di and I (or just me in this case!) help Gran to ice it. And by help, I mostly mean we help to lick the bowl of all the leftover icing! We've always done a lot of baking with Gran and she taught us how to pipe icing; I'm still not as good as her at the writing so you can tell when she's done it (because it's straight and neat) and when I've attempted it (because it'll be wibbly and squished where I run out of space). When we sung happy birthday, as usual my Uncle set about trying to blow the candles out until my Mum sat on him and my Gran put her hand over his mouth! Anyone looking through the window would think we were torturing him!

Di is a huge fan of games so we spent a large portion of the afternoon playing card games. Our favourites are 'Sevens', where there's always someone holding onto cards that stop other people from having their turn and it's infuriating but everyone acts like it's not them. It's amazing how deceptive our family can be! Then there's 'New Market'. We get all of the pennies out of the piggy bank and share them out between us, then you bet on either the Queen of Hearts, Ace of Diamonds, Jack of Spades or King of Clubs and also put a coin in the middle 'pot'. When the cards are dealt, you start with the lowest red and you try to create a run. If you have one of the 'horses' in the middle, if you get to play that card then you get that stash of cash. If you are the first to get rid of all your cards, you win the main pot. The King of Clubs has, for as long as I can remember, been my Gran's nemesis. She so often gets the card in her hand and almost never gets to play it and win the loot! It's so funny and our cheers if it ever happens almost bring the house down!

**Monday 30th November**

Ok, I was not prepared for all of the complaints about the children's Christmas play parts. Some children have come back and changed their minds. "I don't WANT to be Mary", "but I wanted to be a shepherd", "I am NOT wearing that". Tantrums left, right and centre. I tried to care but honestly, I'm still teaching a full curriculum and holding interventions, as well as lunchtime clubs. I tried to convince little Fabio that it's a big deal to be the third camel, but what I really wanted to say is "yes well, LIFE isn't fair". That old chestnut.

It's not just the children! Some parents completely disagreed with a decision and are demanding that their child be the Angel Gabriel instead of a sheep (that one was very accurately placed actually)! The life of a stage director is very stressful. I stuck to my guns and insisted that unless there was a very valid reason, everyone will be keeping their parts thank you very much.

In other news, this is the first time (that I can recall) having a real Christmas tree. It's in the hall and it smells DELIGHTFUL! All the staff stayed until about 7.30pm getting all the decorations up around the school, and TTA and I did a glorious job of grotto-ing the classroom. I think we're wizards. I'm knackered but I'm so excited for the children to see it. Still have to finish up some admin from today though, yawn.

## Tuesday 1st December

Their little faces when they came in and saw the classroom all Christmassy was magical. There were actual gasps and it took so much longer to get to the register because they were so avidly exploring to find all of the Christmas decorations. TTA has even put a Santa brooch on her shirt today! I'm starting the daily rotation of Christmas jewellery and accessories. It's happening. Christmas is coming.

To mark the beginning of December and Christmas decorations arriving, we had a little chat about the meaning behind Christmas. It was really interesting to find out who celebrates Christmas and who doesn't, and obviously the answer to "what is Christmas about" was unanimously "presents", but once we delved a little deeper we got there.

Me: "Some people believe that a very special baby was born on Christmas day who was the son of God."

Jonah: "Oh yeah! I know him!"

Me: "You know him?!"

Jonah: "Yeah! Cheese-us!"

Me: "...Wow yes, almost right well done, it's pronounced Jesus. With a J. That sound J J J."

Jonah: "Yeah. That's what I said. Cheese-us."

Me: (trying really hard not to laugh) "Almost, it's not a ch at the beginning, like cheese, it's a j. Like j for jam. J-esus."

Jonah: "Cheese-us."

We're going to fall out about this soon.

## Wednesday 2nd December

I love December! The glitter is out (much to the daily dismay of the poor cleaners), the mince pies have been put in the staff room and the Christmas production is well under way! We're having to take the children into the hall in groups to practise their scenes as they can't all sit for that long to watch everyone rehearse, but the stage is up and although I'm terrified that someone is going to stage dive off it and break something, it makes it all the more professional looking. I actually found it tricky to be in the staff room instead of with the children today, I just want to be part of all things Christmas all the time!

**Thursday 3rd December**

Me – "Imran, where are your shoes?"
Imran – "Oh I took them off."
Me – "Why?"
Imran – "For comfies."

I love this kid.

Me – "I love this idea but it's not really safe to not wear your shoes. If there was a fire or something and we needed to get out quickly, there wouldn't be time to put your shoes on and then you might hurt your feet outside."
Imran – "I'm always outside without shoes on."
Me – "That's fantastic if that's what you want to do at home, but at school you always need to have your shoes on. Go pop them back on please."
Imran – "Where are they?"

FFS.

Me – "I don't know, sweetheart, where did you leave them?"
Imran – "Where I took them off."
Me – "Well great, they're probably still there?"
Imran – "Oh ok."

REALLY?!

**Friday 4th December**

Another non-uniform day, this time in exchange for donations for the Christmas fair chocolate tombola. Does nobody realise the impact not wearing uniform has on children, their energy and ME!

**Saturday 5th December**

It was my Gran's birthday on Wednesday so the crew came over today. She's 21 again (as she is every year). We went out to Zizzi's (our standard out-of-the-house meal location) for lunch, had a wander round Solihull and then had tea and cake in Drucker's in the afternoon, before going back to the house for actual birthday cake! Not too shabby at all! It seems so funny to me that Gran and Grandad always make the cake, regardless of who's birthday it is. You shouldn't have to make your own cake, but that's just their way I suppose. Di and I decorated it without her though; Di did the writing and it is much, MUCH neater than how I do it! Once again, my uncle tried to blow her candles out so Di wrestled him to give Gran time to do it herself!

**Sunday 6th December**

Basically worked all damn day. Humph. The paperwork and resourcing for this job is insane.

(Bed time: 9pm but couldn't sleep until about 11.30pm)

**Monday 7th December**

The children are getting too comfortable. TTA has, let's say, a very amble bosom for such a short lady, and today, Pippin, a lovely little boy with a thick black country accent and the sweetest personality you can imagine, walked up to her, put his arms around her waist, stared up at her chest and said "oooooh I love your balloons!" I suppose it was an act of appreciation and we laughed HARD at this! Still, boundaries need to be set I think!

**Tuesday 8th December**

TTA - Hey, what stall do you want for the Christmas fair?

Me – I don't know, what are the choices?

TTA - Bash the box, but you have to keep recovering this in wrapping paper. Santa's grotto, but this is always the last thing to finish so you'll be here 'til you're dead. Glitter tattoos, this is a ball ache. Bottle tombola, this is always pretty busy and a good time. Chocolate tombola, this is super busy and tricky to keep up with. Or you can just do the refreshments stall.

Me – Wow that is some insight right there. I guess I'll take the refreshments stall?

TTA – Good choice.

She didn't smile once. She is full of Christmas spirit.

**Wednesday 9th December**

I got a Christmas card from Musaaleh today.
He had written:
"To mis yunwud.
Hapy Crismusaaleh.
From musaaleh"

He must think his name is part of Christmas. Bless him.

**Thursday 10th December**

Phonics is going well. Here's today's:
Me: What sounds are there in ship?
Aryani: Sh-i-t...shit
Inaccurate and offensive; gold star to you, kid.

(Bed time: 10pm!)

**Friday 11th December**

Christmas fair day! It seems quite early but apparently it was booked in case it needed moving. But it didn't need moving. So we're just celebrating Christmas early I suppose.

It turns out that the Christmas fair is so much fun and it used to be on a Saturday but they decided to try it after school today instead, so I've saved myself a weekend day! It did, however, mean a 12 hour end to the week. Santa is a guy they've used for years and has the broadest brummie accent I've ever heard – hilarious. We had Christmas music on in the hall and I wore my Santa hat and jumper and I ate about 12 mince pies. What a lovely time!

Looking around, there were quite a few children having mini meltdowns. They sure cannot handle losing or not getting their way! Either that or the insane amounts of sugar that was being given to children throughout the fair had a huge impact on their emotional stability! I love Christmas.

**Saturday 5th December**

I spent the day with Eddie at his house today watching hour after hour of Trailer Park Boys. The time spent with him.in his room is always chilled and fun, but have I mentioned that he lives with four other guys? All of them adults. All of them with successful careers. Not one of them can wash a plate. There are no clean towels in the bathrooms. There's mould everywhere. I like this guy but I cannot wait for my own place so that I don't have to give myself a full check up every time I've been there.

Eddie is in a heavy metal band and they play quite often. He has some shorts slung over the back of a chair and I don't know how we got on to the subject but he told me they're his gig shorts and that he leaves them out so that they're always ready. Something about this guy just makes me smile. (I was going to say makes my soul smile, but then I thought I might be sick so changed my mind.)

**Sunday 6th December**

You'd think with Christmas approaching there'd be less work to do. There is not. I worked all day again today. I'm getting quicker at planning and getting resources together, but it still takes me such a long time. I have last year's planning to work from but I don't like some of the activities or think there might be a better way to address the learning objective so I spend hours researching different activities. It's not boring but it's so time-consuming.

**Monday 14th December**

We've been rehearsing this stupid Christmas production for a couple of weeks now and I have to say I'm getting more and more impatient that they don't seem to be practising their lines and four of them still haven't brought in their costumes ready for the dress rehearsal. Have we got a seating plan? Is it being recorded this year? Do the lights even work anymore? The Christmas tree has fallen over. Has anyone seen the Elf on the Shelf? I hate Christmas. Oh also, I've got to submit the end of term class data by the end of this week. When is that supposed to happen! It made me realise just how much teaching and learning time we sacrificed to practise that one scene with Mary, Joseph and the innkeeper 348 times. When's the last time we did Phonics? Oh who cares about Phonics when Angel Gabriel keeps getting stage fright! How on earth do you balance Christmas joy with all the other stuff that still needs doing?

We had the first performance this afternoon and after all of the worry, it was just beautiful, I nearly cried! Most of the children actually did cry. It must be intimidating to have those professional lights blinding you and a million adults staring at you. We had a few have little break downs and Mary tripped and dropped Jesus, a camel knocked the inn set down and the speakers stopped working at one point. I need a nap.

What was lovely is how many parents came over to say how wonderful it was and to thank TTA and me. That was really touching. People don't often tell you when you're doing a good job, I've noticed. Just when they're not happy about something, so getting compliments is so appreciated. Shame I can't be equally as forthcoming about my views on each of their parenting styles.

**Tuesday 15th December**

Christmas production number two was at 9.30am this morning. This was a much better rendition than yesterday afternoon, except for the end. Yesterday, everyone who had a parent or carer there to watch just went home early and the rest of us had an extended story time (we lost count of the yawns...). Today, however, we had to do the rest of the day in school. This did not go down well. They're tired anyway, they probably had a huge come down from the adrenaline and then their parents or carers waltzed off and left them again, so there were tears and hysterics and tantrums. Life is real hard, you guys.

(Bed time: 9pm)

**Wednesday 16th December**

Christmas party day. Oh my God. Absolute mania. It's baffling how we asked children (or rather, their parents) to bring in **light** picnic food for their afternoon party, yet an hour after having lunch, they're sitting down to an extra feast! Don't get me wrong, this is like a dream for me, but I'm not sure it's great to overfeed small children, especially when you're asking them to play party games like Musical Bumps! Each child had brought an entire second lunchbox for this picnic and I'm amazed none of them popped.

We'd asked them to bring party clothes to change into so that they're energy is at an ever so slightly lower level coming in, but I was not well enough braced for all of the volume, tears and joy spilling out of them for the entire duration of the party. We had to address the sore losers in the group – even when we played pass the parcel where everyone's a winner! When Betty got a green keyring when she really wanted a blue one oh boy did we see some tantrums.

It's so hard to try to 'control' a Christmas party. You want everyone to have a great time, to party, to dance, to eat, to let loose, but the trouble is...children can't always handle that. With a huge burst of excitement, there is the come down. The inevitable inability to handle a couple of hours of pure fun. This is where we'd planned the little snack to help or perhaps a story, but I suppose it would be like going to a friend's party and halfway through being asked to calm down! Such a tricky balance, but in the end, my job is to keep them safe, and letting them jump around for two hours whilst eating sweets and belting out Christmas tunes is the antithesis of safe.

Their party clothes, though! For lots of children it was just jeans and a Christmas jumper, totally fine. But for some it meant an entire three-piece suit complete with bowtie, or a puffy dress made entirely of sequins that you can hear coming before you see it. Priceless.

I wouldn't want to have missed this, but I am a bit cross that we don't get our non-contact time this week. Just because it's the last week of term, it doesn't mean that we don't have an entire term to plan for, or assessment data to look over, pupil progress meetings to prepare for. This doesn't seem well thought through. I was going to say it isn't fair but it makes me sound like a child!

**Thursday 17th December**

Christmas lunch day!

1. I need someone to explain chocolate cracknel to me. Everyone got so excited but I'm not a fan, which is surprising because I LOVE chocolate.
2. Why on earth would you put custard on top of chocolate cracknel? You're a maniac if you do this.

On another, more important note, I am absolutely overwhelmed at the generosity of families who have been bringing me Christmas cards and presents! I did a little goodie bag for the children from me and TTA with some reindeer food and some little activities, but gosh have some of the parents gone to town! There were chocolates, bottles of wine, some homemade cakes (um SUPER sweet thought but I ain't touching no cake that's had kid's fingers in!), a lovely seaside-y bracelet, some body spray (am I 12?), some candles and a couple of mugs. This is just so lovely. I got a bit emotional when they started handing me presents, and so many of them had got similar things for TTA too. I feel warm inside.

**Friday 18th December**

Woohoo Christmas holibobs! It was Christmas jumper day and I was so excited, until upon opening the door I had a very mardy parent moan about how they're being expected to pay for so many things and provide costumes for everything. I said we were under the assumption that most people would have a Christmas top of some sort, or something green or red that they could wear. To which she had another go at me about having to buy him clothes! Hey, don't have kids if you don't want to pay to clothe them! My response was "yes, children are very expensive to have aren't they". That may have crossed the line, but for goodness sake.

Blake had a couple of tantrums today but we were able to calm him down pretty quickly and distract him with some plastic dinosaurs, which he loves. Thank goodness (again) for TTA, I don't know how I'd cope with him if I was by myself, I'm often quite worried for the other children and find that I'm watching him all the time in case I need to intervene.

Anyway, we went into the hall for the last part of the afternoon with the rest of the school for a candlelit carol concert which was divine, and a whole school trying to keep up with the words and actions to the 12 Days of Christmas is the funniest thing I've seen yet! I'm completely shattered and am committed to not doing any work at all over the Christmas break to reset for the new year.

**<u>Sunday 20th December</u>**

Yesterday basically consisted of eating, sleeping, watching Christmas specials and whatsapping with Eddie. A couple of other people have started using whatsapp with me instead of messaging and I'm livid! For so long it's been just Eddie's way to talk to me. Urgh what a sap I'm becoming.

**<u>Monday 21st December</u>**

No children. No noise. No Phonics. Just me. I already love this week. I had the day to myself today, seeing as Mum was out at work, so I got all the presents I've bought out on the floor in the lounge, poured myself a Malibu and coke, stacked up some mince pies and wrapped the presents whilst watching Christmas films. I love this day, I do it every year and it gives me so much joy. It hurts my back though, and whilst I can see the appeal for my bodily health to do this activity at the dining room table, it's not quite the same as sprawling out on the floor. Sorry spine.

**Tuesday 22nd December**

I played Santa today! I had a couple of dates with friends (Christmas Costa, lunch, mooching in the shops etc.) but mostly spent the day dishing out the presents I'd wrapped yesterday. There were carol singers in the town centre and every shop, restaurant and café had gorgeous Christmas decorations. I love this time of year! Though it rained really hard and I got wet foot from accidently stepping off a curb into a ridiculous puddle. I couldn't help but think, if only this were snow, it would be so magical. Then I remembered I hate snow and probably wouldn't have left the house had it been snowing as hard as it was raining. Ah Christmas cheer!

**Wednesday 23rd December**

It's so funny having divorced parents around Christmas time, because everyone (literally everyone) seems to think that it's the best thing ever to get two lots of presents, two Christmas mornings, two Christmas dinners etc. What it actually means, is weeks of planning as to who is seeing whom on what day. When my sister and I were kids, we used to spend Christmas eve and Christmas morning with one parent, then the rest of Christmas day and boxing day with the other, swapping year to year. At some point in our teenage years, our parents decided to pass the responsibility over to us, declaring "it's up to you who you spend Christmas with, your choice!" To avoid any tricky decisions we soon came up with a system that meant we would have two Christmases. We would have one day with each parent and just alternate who we spent actual Christmas day with and who got another designated day. It works fine, going back and forth, although it's quite tiring it means we get more quality time with both parents and they both LOVE Christmas so it's always a fun time with each of them.

This year, I'm at home with Mum until boxing day and Di is coming to stay with us tomorrow, then Di and I will pop up to Dad's on Monday and have a couple of days there. Dad always goes nuts with decorations and his house lights up like the Blackpool illuminations! I do like having a whole day with each parent, it's so much nicer than having to get up and go somewhere on Christmas day. Mostly because we start drinking at about 10am!

**Thursday 24th December**

I spent the whole day at home on the sofa, watching Christmas films and eating yule log. Thank goodness we bought another one for actual Christmas! Mum and I did some food prep for lunch tomorrow. My grandparents and Uncle are coming tomorrow for lunch onwards, which I'm so excited about. We used to go to my Mum's cousin's house on Boxing Day with loads of the family and I always remember playing The Ring Game. One person stands in the middle, whilst the others spread out in a circle around them holding on to a piece of string that has a ring threaded on to it. You have your hands grasping the string at all times and the idea is to keep the ring moving round the circle without the person in the middle seeing it. They have to guess who's holding it. My Uncle is one to avoid standing next to in this game! He always gets really nervous and makes 'nooo' sort of noises when the ring comes towards him and will hold his hands (and the string) up high to avoid the ring being able to get passed to him! It's absolutely hilarious and most of the time we all end up on the floor laughing. My sister likes us to play it still so we might give that a go tomorrow, though it gives me anxiety!

I'm not sure what other people do on Christmas Eve, but I still like to be in bed before 'Santa' can arrive. I know it's childish and that my friends are out having drinks or having little parties, but I'm a big fan of a tradition so I still like to pop to bed before midnight! It also means I can wake up earlier for presents! I've been thinking about this and how funny it is that young children are up at the crack of dawn to open their presents as they can't hold their excitement any longer. Then you become a teenager and might rock up when lunch is being served. Now, as a 21 year old, I wake up at a normal time, but it's my Mum who is often coming in to me all excited about it being Christmas!

Apparently there was a time when I was very young, and I woke up to see that Santa had not been. I was an absolute wreck, but when my Mum came up to see why I was crying, she informed me it was only 11pm.

**Monday 28th December**

Allow me to write this diary entry in Bridget Jones style, to summarise the last few days and really capture the spirit of what I've been up to.
Yule logs eaten – at least 3
Mince pies eaten – minimum 4,000
Malibu and cokes drunk – about 5 per day in my pint-sized, fast food replica drinks holder with Santa on the side (holidays are coming!)
Family arguments – 1. Someone gets very stressed cooking Christmas dinner and yells the instructions.
Christmas dinners - 2
Naps per day – at least 3
Carols sung – all of them
Christmas films watched – we've completed Netflix
Hours spent whatsapping Eddie – about 90% of them

Di and I are driving up to see Padre in the Lakes tomorrow and Christmas number 2 shall commence on Wednesday! The list of food he sent us that he's bought is extensive, I am SO excited!

**Thursday 31st December**

I love it up here. It's so quiet and peaceful and it's been snowing so it's just beautiful. We've had quite a few snowy walks through the fields and it's just my all time favourite place to be. Except in a field of cows. They're terrifying. They stare at you hard and you know that if they came at you, you'd be finished. Dad likes to make fun of me for being nervous of cows but they can be so vicious! The farm up the road has cows and every so often we make it up here when they have calves and they're just so cute.

With it being New Years Eve in the countryside, there's not a whole lot to do, so we're going to Dad's neighbours' house for dinner and drinks. It's a farmer and his wife and she makes the BEST banoffee pie I've ever tasted, probably because farmers don't dabble in reduced fat content. It's not very Christmassy so I doubt she'll have made one for tonight but whatever else is there will be delicious.

**Friday 1st January**

It's so strange to be an adult (of sorts) and to hang out with other adults but feel so much like a child in their presence. Dad often likes us to hang out with his friends and can't quite seem to understand why it's not our favourite thing to do! Last night was fun at times though. We played giant snakes and ladders and when everyone is a couple of glasses deep it's quite funny watching people count their way round a board! Today has been spent in much of a food/alcohol hangover. I love Christmas so much, but as soon as NYE has come and gone I immediately want rid of it all. Except yule log. I could eat that all year round.

(Bed times have been successfully pushed back to at least midnight as I'm not getting up until about 10am every day)

**Sunday 3rd January**

Eddie's lot were having a house party last night so I went over. At one point we were in the kitchen dancing like idiots to a Tech 9 song that I haven't heard before because I'm not that cool. All I can remember are the lyrics "and drinkin', and smokin', and humpin', and likin' it" and I wonder if this will become our song...

I'm so gutted to be going back to work tomorrow. I know I'm so lucky to have had two weeks off as some people worked the whole time or just managed to get a couple of days, so I'm really grateful for the time. But urgh. It's hard enough going in after a weekend but after two weeks off, especially two hectic, busy weeks, it's so much worse. I think I'm more tired than when term ended!

# Chapter 3
# Spring term 1

**Monday 4th January**

The spring term is a bit of a strange one. It's winter. It will be winter for another two and a half months. But we're a third of the way through the year (which I cannot believe) so it's called the spring term. Wow a third of the year... I've been a teacher for a third of a year! We have done one out of three terms. One term down, two to go.

I miss the Christmas holidays. Everything is so bare and cold. Though it's one of the reasons I love working in a school so much; we still have colourful displays and fun role plays and it doesn't have to be a boring office.

The parents were invited in for a special assembly today to celebrate all of the children who had 100% attendance in the Autumn term. I felt really bad that I wasn't part of the club, even though there were no awards for staff. Though I've heard of a headteacher who created a staff attendance board in the hall for everyone to see to encourage staff to come to work. This just sounds horrific to me, I was off for genuine reasons and if I had forced myself to come whilst I was that poorly I would have been so much worse and taken down a load of other people with me, so a public board shaming me for being ill would be the worst! There's a lot of stigma around taking time off. There's guilt and shame and people are almost considered weak or failures if they need to take time off sick. I wonder if it's worse for teachers because we have so much holiday, but nobody should be made to feel like they should work when they're not well. Plus, they just give it to everyone else!

**Tuesday 5th January**

Despite everyone coming in happy and energetic yesterday, two children cried when they came in this morning. I feel their pain. I want to be at home on the sofa watching films all day for the rest of my life too, kids.

**Wednesday 6th January**

Having a Wednesday out of class really helps the week go by. Monday you get up all full of life (and dread), Tuesday is a little bit tricky and you're sleepier, but then Wednesday is no children and just lovely paperwork. It gives me such a great mid-week break and it helps Thursday and Friday go by a bit easier. I steamed ahead with my planning today and managed to get it all done. I feel so good when I've been so productive and I almost felt bad going back into the classroom all jolly and full of energy when TTA and the cover teacher are on their knees!

**Thursday 7th January**

I'm tired today. Real tired. I think I peaked yesterday. I got TTA to do all of the adult led stuff whilst I 'observed' the children for assessment purposes. I love my job.

(Bed time: back to 9.30pm. It feels right)

**Friday 8th January**

This morning I had a pupil progress meeting with the head to talk about, funnily enough, the progress of all the children in my class. I haven't done one of these before and it was a bit intimidating, there was so much paperwork to prepare for it ahead of time. I had to use the data put into the system before Christmas to work out percentages about how many children are below, at or above where they should be for each subject, as well as where they're at in terms of progress. It's absolutely soul crushing. You spend each and every day personalising learning for each individual based on their circumstances, I know every single one of them so well, but then you put the data in and they become a statistic, a number. Ooh you've only got 72% of children on track for where they should be for Reading. This isn't good enough, what are you doing to ensure this is at least 90%? Well, of the other 28% that are slightly below where they should be, most of them speak English as an additional language, two have pretty significant special needs, one has mega attendance issues, three don't read at all at home, I could go on. I have an intervention plan for all of them, they're all making great progress but that doesn't matter because they're still behind where they should be with their attainment. It's infuriating.

Has anyone told the government and Ofsted that children are not robots? Perhaps they won't all follow the exact same path or pace when they're learning? Perhaps we don't reduce children down to percentages, instead we look at them as individuals, which is what we are trained to do in the first instance.

Once we'd gone through everything we're doing for these children, there were no suggestions about what else we could do or anything that we're missing, so clearly TTA and I know what we're doing, but it's not good enough. We need to cast some magic over these children to bring them up to where they 'should' be. It's only January!

**Saturday 9th January**

I went for my first mortgage meeting today. I do not understand finance at all. This is not a surprise to me, but I think my Mum was a bit shocked at how long it took me to grasp interest rates and repayment schedules and good lord it's going to take forever to pay it back! I think I'll be dead before I get it paid off. But I have a decision in principle along with my savings for a deposit so I'm a bit more clear as to what I can afford and I'm pleasantly surprised. Bring on the house hunt!

**Sunday 10th January**

Mortgages yesterday and work today. What a joyful January weekend.

**Monday 11th January**

Oh my goodness, the funniest and least funny thing happened today. Sandeep has osteoporosis so he is really delicate, and having been premature he's also pretty tiny. I remember at the beginning of the year, his parents telling me that if we lifted him up off the floor by his arms, they'd just pop right out of their sockets. Yikes. So we've been super careful with him so far and he often needs a little bit more time and attention when we're moving around etc., but this is fine because he's lovely... not that it wouldn't be fine if he wasn't lovely, I just might silently huff more.

Today, he told me he needed the toilet and so off he went. I helped him get set up and then I loitered outside in the corridor just in case, which I was glad about when he screamed for help. I went running in and burst out laughing! Poor Sandeep was folded up in half inside the toilet, having fallen in butt first, his legs and arms up above his head! He also found it quite funny, which I'm relieved about because I was really laughing, but it was an effort between TTA and me to get him out without pulling on any body part too hard. I will never forget the sight of a child literally folded in half inside a toilet bowl!

**Tuesday 12th January**

The wind has got a lot to answer for. It's worse than all the other weathers put together for riling children up for absolutely no reason at all. They're louder, more boisterous, more excitable and less interested in Maths than ever. Apparently horses are the same... I wonder what the science is there.

**Wednesday 13th January**

I went over to do handover at the end of the day and it was awful. Everything was going fine, despite the weather being horrible (it's so much harder to recognise who is collecting whom when there are umbrellas and hoods everywhere) until two parents came to me with Isadora and Jonah. These two children are great friends and so are their parents. They're always together so it wasn't a surprise to see them together. When I let the children out of the classroom, I ask them to point at who they're going with so that I can check who it is and know that they're safe.

On this occasion, however, it appeared that Jonah had gone out to his mum and Isadora had followed soon afterwards, and because I know them to be together a lot I hadn't checked carefully enough because Isadora's mum wasn't actually there, she was round the corner collecting her older daughter. Luckily, Isadora had gone straight round and found her, but her mum came back to tell me. She was so lovely about it, but Jonah's mum started yelling at me. It wasn't even her kid! So I tried to ignore her and kept apologising to Isadora's mum and had a chat with Isadora to say how important it is that she only goes if she sees her mum, but Jonah's mum kept yelling at me. Now, I don't take pride in the fact that I have a really short temper, but I do, and I held out for as long as I could by saying things like "excuse me I'll sort this out with Isadora's mum" but in the end I shouted back at her. She's been really rude the whole year so far so I just lost it.

I went down to the headteacher after they had left (and I'd calmed down) to tell her that she might be getting a complaint about me; Jonah's mum is very well known to the school for being a tricky parent, but there was no excuse for me sinking to her level. I might try not to come back for handover on Wednesdays from now on, this is clearly a sign!

**Thursday 14th January**

Apparently, because it's so busy around Christmas, we save the pantomime treat for January. This. Is. Awesome. The whole afternoon was spent in the hall watching Robin Hood, laughing at jokes that the children didn't get and wondering how these actors keep their energy up for so long. TTA pointed out that we do a similar job, always having to be 'on', but with less costume changes throughout the day. Unless someone wees themselves whilst sitting on your lap, then you need a costume change super quick. Funnily enough, Blake was super well behaved today so TTA managed to watch the whole thing too; you can never tell how he's going to react to something new, though we have been warning him all week that this was coming and would be a change in the routine so maybe that helped to prepare him.

The really fun bit was when I had absolutely checked out of what was happening in the hall until I saw all of my class pointing and me, cheering and clapping. I wondered what had prompted such a sudden surge of appreciation for me, so I smiled and nodded at them. That nod accepted their nomination for me to enter a dance contest. Good God. Me and one of the year two teachers reluctantly went up to the front and had to dance to Baby Shark. I had no idea this was even a thing and once again felt so out of touch with the very age group I was supposed to be an expert in! It was declared a draw and I've been singing the song ever since. It's really catchy. Must remember to pay attention at all times.

**<u>Friday 15th January</u>**

I've discovered my favourite way to tell children off. It's through a reflection where they can't see you. They think they're so clever having hidden away in a corner of the room, under the cover of some shelves or the role play tent. But from where I was sat, I could see them in the reflection of the window. When Imran and Gary starting having a competition to see how many things they could fit into their pants (true story), I gently called over to them to consider hygiene and whether it was fair on everyone else. I could see them looking around to see how I could see them and when they peeked out from behind the shelves I gave them my teacher look. They apologised and I almost couldn't contain my mirth! Well done, windows.

**<u>Saturday 16th January</u>**

It's official – Eddie and I are a couple! It's taken us long enough but we had the conversation and changed our status' on Facebook, so that means it's real. I don't think I've stopped smiling all day.

**<u>Sunday 17th January</u>**

I've just had one of those days. I did some baking and somehow ended up with butter on the kitchen window, I tried to defrost some frozen fruit in the microwave and a raspberry caught fire, then when I couldn't find my keys, they turned up in the fridge. Something has gone wrong in my mind tank.

**Monday 18th January**

It's not necessarily an early years requirement, but we've started PE lessons. This class is generally pretty well-behaved, calm, and mostly well-mannered, but let me tell you, as soon as I took them into the hall for a PE lesson, every single one of them turned feral. Feral.

I kid you not, they tiptoed up the corridor with their arms by their sides, creeping past the deputy headteacher's office because I told them she might breathe fire if she hears them coming; they were grinning and cute. Then I opened the door to the hall and it was like they were possessed! They immediately ran as fast as they could in all directions and shouted and screamed and spun round and started pile on's. Good Lord, what happened to my gorgeous class of angels and who replaced them with these savages?

Even when I managed to get them settled and gave them a good talking to, when I asked them to get into a space they did that thing which has been done for centuries where you stand with your arms out and swing them round to check that you're in a good space. Classic.

I'll have to sort this out for next week. That hall has magical powers. Evil magical powers.

**Tuesday 19th January**

It's due to snow tonight. I have some feelings about this. Snow is awesome, when it's Christmas time and it's gentle and pretty and you feel like you're in a Raymond Briggs cartoon. I hate the snow, however. I'm one of those people. No I don't want to build a snowman, I don't want numb, wet hands, I don't want to go walking in it and I absolutely do not want to drive to and from work with ice and sludge all over the place. Snow can politely get lost. (Grumpy, table for one.)

(Bed time: 9.30pm but stayed awake worrying about the snow)

**Wednesday 20th January**

Oh boy did it snow last night! I woke up this morning to quite a pile of snow all around the house (is pile the right term for a lot of snow?) and immediately started dreading my journey to work just as I was last night. Stupid snow. Did I mention that it's cold and wet? There's a good chance any normal person will fall over in it so that goes double for clumsy old me, plus people think it's ok to throw it at your face! This is not ok. The journey was fine in the end, of course, plus our wonderful site manager had been out since the middle of the night (5am ish?) shovelling the pathways clear; what an absolute gem. The school looked so pretty with snow all over it, but I was nervous about the playground at break time!

Reception has its own little play area and when they went out for morning break, I walked over for a little bit of fresh air from working in the staff room for PPA all morning. When I got there, Clive was standing underneath the climbing frame, swinging around the fireman's pole. It shook about a foot of snow off the top of the climbing frame which all landed on him with a thud. Don't judge me, but I laughed so hard. I mean, I nearly fell over laughing. Like Dasha and her knock-knock joke, I could barely breathe for laughing. Right in his face. It was only when I looked up and saw his shocked little eyes staring at me that I remembered I was a teacher and should probably check if he was ok. (He was, just very surprised and cold.) I really don't think he found it funny, but if I had caught that on video I would definitely get £250 from You've Been Framed.

**Thursday 21st January**

Blake threw a chair at me again today. We had been reading a book together and he seemed calm and happy. He said he wanted to read by himself so I told him I was really proud of his reading and had really enjoyed our time together in the book corner. Literally thirty seconds later he was screaming and throwing books around the room and as I went over to him he screwed up his face like he wanted to kill me and picked up the nearest chair and threw it at me. We had to evacuate the rest of the children while he continued to trash the classroom. He had torn up the book he was looking at so I assume he came across a word he didn't know or a plot point he didn't like. I've got quite a few bruises from today and I was shaking for ages afterwards. He got sent home as they decided he was too fragile to come back in to tidy the classroom, even though it's recommended that children put things right after something like this. So another lovely TA came in to help me sort it out whilst TTA kept the children entertained in the hall with some stories and I sobbed the entire time.

The hardest part was when the class came back in to the classroom. A few were asking questions, one had been crying since the incident started, a couple had even been sniggering like a child having a meltdown was funny. I'm guessing all of this amounted to the fact that they just didn't know how to handle what they'd seen, but the trouble is, neither did I. I was so scared for them, for myself, for Blake. So confused as to what had happened and how it had happened so quickly following a really nice interaction. I didn't know how to explain it to them but knew I had to as this was obviously not going to stop. I talked to them about how tricky it is for all of us to recognise and deal with our emotions and how some people find it harder than others. I tried to explain how feeling upset or angry is normal and nothing to be afraid of, but that how we deal with those emotions is really important and that's what we're all trying to learn how to do this year. I encouraged them to ask questions and lots of them did so hopefully I answered them in some sort of helpful way.

I remember working with children who struggled with their emotions whilst on placement throughout my training but it was nothing like this. We've called an Educational Psychologist to come and assess him. Hopefully they can help. I feel really out of my depth here.

**Friday 22nd January**

My bruises from yesterday had a growth spurt overnight. I've got a lovely purple one on my arm, a huge one on my shin and a scary one around my collar bone. I've got a massive scratch on my face too, which I hadn't noticed yesterday. I've worn clothes that hide the bruises and covered the scratch as well as I could with makeup.

I had three parents ask on the door this morning to talk to me about Blake. They were all very calm but I can see how worried they are. I didn't feel qualified to reassure them. I didn't sleep very well, I kept waking up anxious and wondering what today would be like. I tried my best to discuss what's going on without crossing the line and talking about someone else's child, but suggested to all three of them that the head or deputy would be happy to talk to them if they felt it necessary, just to ensure they didn't feel like I was fobbing them off. What can you say?

He came in really happy again this morning. No mention of yesterday, which is probably best so that we're not reminding him of something horrible that happened, but I have to say I found it a little bit difficult to smile and pretend that nothing had happened. I could see a couple of children were a bit wary of him today. We need to be careful of this, I don't want him to be alienated in the classroom. Loneliness is not a helpful feeling when you already struggle to handle negativity. I stuck to him like glue today. He had a couple of moments but I managed to distract him before he majorly kicked off. I went to speak to the head about this and suggest that he needs a 1:1 support as neither TTA nor I can spend the rest of the year like this as it will take us away from the other children. She said we don't have the budget and that we're doing fine so we'll just carry on. I tried to tell her how anxious we all are and that it doesn't feel 'fine', but she just repeated that we're here for the children and he comes first and that everything is ok. It's funny how she thinks everything is ok, yet she's not in the classroom dealing with him and worrying about him constantly. Must be nice.

I left at 3.45pm today. My head hurts, my collar bone is throbbing and I'm exhausted from worrying all day. Screw next week, I'll deal with it on Monday. I just need a break.

**Saturday 23rd January**

I was exhausted last night; poor Mum was horrified at the state I came home in and I fell asleep about 7pm. I had horrible nightmares though and couldn't sleep past about 1am. I've just been napping and crying and not really knowing what to do with myself all day.

**Sunday 24th January**

I cannot tell you how badly I do not want to go into work tomorrow. I went out with a couple of mates today but I couldn't concentrate and couldn't find any joy in what we were doing. They were really sympathetic when I gave them a really basic overview of what's been happening, but the trouble with telling people is that they want to fix it for you. Which is lovely but it's just not really possible. I've thought all the thoughts about refusing to go in, demanding more staff or more training etc. but I can't do any of it. I can't choose who I teach and who I don't so I listen and I nod and I thank people for their suggestions but I know I can't do much about it other than keep a behaviour log and keep bugging senior leadership for help.

**Monday 25th January**

I barely slept again last night and I had a panic attack on the way into work this morning. I can't remember having had a proper panic attack before and it was awful. I was crying in the car, really dangerous to drive that way, thinking about how Blake was going to be when he came in this morning and how I was going to deal with it and ended up having to pull over because I was hyperventilating. I managed to make it into the classroom but had to switch the lights off, close the door and hide for a bit until my panic subsided. It was horrific, I was really scared. TTA was a bit late this morning as she got stuck in traffic, so she ended up coming in with the children. She took one look at me, narrowed her eyes and asked if I was ok. I had to look away and use a sing-song voice to tell her yes so that I wouldn't start crying again. She walked off, made me a hot chocolate and didn't say anything else, but I noticed her checking on me a lot more today. If I haven't mentioned it before, I'll say it now, I'm SO grateful for her. I was desperate to let last week go and start fresh but it's easier said than done. No huge incidents with Blake today, so I won't dwell on him further.

PE went better today because I controlled the mania! I set up two mats right by the door of the hall and asked them to sit on a mat as soon as we went in and counted them down to get us in there in 15 seconds or less. It sounds so clinical and boring writing it down like this, but it worked! They loved the time challenge, got in and sat down so quickly, then I called them by name to move in a particular way (crawl, hop, roll etc.) to a space I gave them, making sure they concentrated by saying they couldn't repeat a movement that had already been used. I'm a genius. By the end, the children were getting so creative with how they moved and I got really jealous of how flexible they all are! Dasha goes to gymnastics classes and although she's built pretty sturdily, she can bend in all sorts of ways I don't understand!

It got to about 2pm and Johnathan pointed out that my stomach was making noises and I realised I hadn't eaten all day. I nailed a bunch of chocolates from the cupboard after school, but I must make sure I'm more prepared with food in the future as this is a regular occurrence at work!

**Tuesday 26th January**

I've realised that however much I know about children, their development, their needs, their barriers to learning and how to motivate them, I have absolutely no idea what they're talking about when the talk about their toys. They keep mentioning programmes and building sets and all sorts of things that I have to google! I'm actually having to google what children are saying to me. This is insane. I'm so old. I thought it was bad enough that I don't understand Snapchat or TikTok and I don't see how 'reels' are any different from a video, but apparently it's just not millennials that I'm out of touch with. It's the generation I've based my entire degree and career on!

**Wednesday 27th January**

You know what's a great idea? Offering to read the children a bedtime story at school so that their parents don't need to find babysitters for them while they come and listen to an information evening. You know what's not a great idea? Offering to read the children a bedtime story at school so that their parents don't need to find babysitters for them while they come and listen to an information evening.

In theory it's fantastic. It was so cute to see so many children come back to school at 6.30pm in their pjs with a cuddly toy. Offering them squash and a biscuit, and one for me of course. Lovely. Yes let's read a couple of stories because your parents will only be in the hall for half an hour. After 45 minutes, they're bored and tired, your throat is getting sore because, oh yeah, you've already been talking since 7.30 this morning and suddenly you're working another 13 hour day.

The parents that came are the ones that would've read a letter we sent out with this information on. The others clearly didn't even bother to read this letter, despite me reminding them yesterday.

I'm tired and grumpy. What's new. It's a good job it happened to fall on my non-contact day though. It felt easier having not been with the children all day. That sounds so awful but it's so exhausting!

**Thursday 28th January**

Frasier drew a picture of an elephant today...

I need to teach more art.

**<u>Friday 29th January</u>**
An educational psychologist came in today to observe Blake. She basically said the same things as the behaviour lead. We've ordered a tent. I still don't feel particularly supported.

**<u>Saturday 30th January</u>**
I cried a lot again today. I feel quite hopeless. This isn't what I thought teaching would be like.

**<u>Sunday 31st January</u>**
I took Eddie to look at a couple of houses with me today and there's one I am really excited about! He's been so great about Blake, he just hugs me real tight and I feel so much safer and better. I'm going to book a second viewing for that house.

**<u>Monday 1st February</u>**
It's National Storytelling week and Children's Mental Health week. What a week! Both are things I am really into. We're going to have stories galore and do lots of activities on how to deal with our emotions, lots of yoga and mindfulness and I'm hoping it will be as

good for me and TTA and it is for them! It's come at such a needed time.

**Tuesday 2nd February**

Getting free fruit from the government is awesome, but we've been getting a lot of bananas recently and there are a lot of bananaphobes in this class. So, to make it more interesting, every time we announce what the fruit is going to be for that day and it's bananas, I've started doing a little jig and singing "iiiiiiiiit's bananaramas!" It's worked and more children are now eating, and loving, bananas. I have, however, inadvertently created a group of children who now thing that bananas are called bananaramas. I must remember how influential they are.

**Wednesday 3rd February**

Frances' Nan used to be a primary school teacher. I saw her this morning on my way out of the classroom to the staff room for my non-contact time and she offered to come in a couple of times a week in the morning to listen to some children read! What a lovely person. YES PLEASE! I might put this out in a notice and see if anyone else wants to come and help.

**Thursday 4th February**

We were tidying up today and Johnathan brought me a screwed up bit of paper as big as his thumbnail.

"Yes Johnathan?"

"I found this."

"...Ok, where do you think you should put a piece of rubbish?"

Literally 5 minutes go by.

"In the bin?"

"Yes please!"

It's like we haven't been in this classroom tidying up every day for 5 months.

(Bed time: 9pm and I'll be honest, it felt late)

**Friday 5th February**

I've had so many offers of help from parents and family members! YES! Jonah's Mum came in this morning to read with some children and stayed for about an hour. As she was leaving, she said "I've always thought this job is really easy but I didn't realised everything you have to deal with. Hats off to you." Ding ding ding! Give this woman a microphone and let her spread that message. Isn't it funny how people don't necessarily understand what they've never done? Isn't it funny how having two children at home is completely different from having 30 in a classroom?! It was quite nerve-racking having a parent come in because I thought she would just watch me and judge me, but it turned out really well!

**Saturday 6th February**

I fell over three times today. You know when you trip on nothing? I did that. Three times. The Wii Fit was right about me.

**Sunday 7th February**

It was Grandparent day again today! None of us wanted to do much because it's been such horrible weather. So Grandad and I played Majhong on his computer and Gran, Di and I did some baking; jam tarts YUM! My Mum had also bought us some fizzy sweets for the journey which we dared my Uncle to eat; he's incredibly sensitive when it comes to sour food and he was on the floor in seconds, his face scrunched up so tight! The poor thing, he was probably really hating it but boy did we laugh!

**Monday 8th February**

I am beginning to learn that children are gross. Inside and out. They're disgusting. Other people who have had their own children have probably already made this discovery. They have probably already experienced beans in places that children shouldn't have beans. Naïve little me used to think that they are super cute. Not always, dear misguided teacher, not always. They eat stuff they shouldn't eat, they pick stuff they have no business picking, they'll scratch anything right in your face and they are totally fine with letting everything out in front of anyone. I suppose in a way it's quite freeing. If your teacher calls to you "Bernard, come on, everyone is outside..." and you're happy to shout back "I'M POOING" then fair play to you! This happened today and I had no response, what do you say to that? Carry on? Sorry to have disturbed you? You've got this? Probably just 'ok' will do it. There's no need to respond further to that.

**<u>Tuesday 9th February</u>**

My Dad is one of 8 children. Apparently, on pancake day when he was a child, all 8 children would stand in a line with their plates, and my Nan would make pancake after pancake. Each child would get theirs, go to the table and eat, then re-join the back of the line. This is what my day felt like! 30 pancakes! On top of this, it was time for parents' evenings round 2. This was not clever planning on my part!

Generally tonight was easier than the first round of parents' evenings. I'm still exhausted, having done a 13 hour day, but the relationships are a bit more built up with the parents now so it feels easier to know how to approach each family. I had some really wonderful comments from parents who are happy and keen for their child to do well and supporting them at home.

Then I had Betty's Mum. Betty doesn't read at home. Her reading diary is always empty apart from when TTA or I write in it. I said to her that Betty is really struggling with reading and that she needs to be reading every day. Her response was "oh, ok, so does that mean she's getting 1:1 support at school now?" I felt like saying, "no, you bellend, I mean you. YOU read with your own child!" But I refrained. I said "no, we don't have the staff for that, I meant she needs to be reading at home every day. I've noticed her diary is often empty." She told me that she works full time and her mother, Betty's Grandmother, has her after school. Again, my brain came out with "Is your mother illiterate?" but luckily my mouth paraphrased; "oh fantastic, so she could read with Betty after school every day?" I think she wanted to kill me but grudgingly agreed. I told her I was looking forward to reading Betty's diary every day to see what she and her Grandmother had been reading. I hope she's not into voodoo, otherwise I might be in trouble.

**Wednesday 10th February**

You know what's awkward? Talking about how shit a child is at something while they're in the room. That's awkward. I know some parents can't get childcare for parents' evenings and need to bring the child with them, but Katerina is an only child so she didn't even have any siblings with her to make any noise. So we're all in the same room, she's sat in the book corner in silence 'reading' a book (staring at us over the top of it) and I'm trying to communicate to her parents that whilst she is absolutely lovely and tries really hard, she needs more work on her speech and language skills. I was diplomatic and as quiet as I could be, but she definitely heard and in the end, I brought her over to talk about some of the fun games and activities I was suggesting she play at home with her parents.

Blake's parents evening was conducted with the deputy so I had some backup. His parents are still denying there are any sort of problem. It's infuriating because I'm sure there's more we could be doing to identify the issues and put strategies into place to help him if they just acknowledged it. I'm not a parent so I have to try really hard to see it from their side, and I can imagine that he either doesn't behave at home like he does in school (which I know isn't the case because I've seen how he treats his parents in the playground) or they just don't want to accept that there's something not quite right. It was a really tricky conversation and I just wish we could all be on the same page to help him.

**Thursday 11th February**

Teaching isn't a real job. Teaching isn't a real job? I saw this lovely thread on Twitter today. WHO ARE YOU?! Who is saying this?! What does this even mean?! Are millions of adults around the country, no, the world, going into schools and just hiding in a cupboard all day? Nope! Of course it's a real job, and I dare anyone who thinks this to go and try it for themselves.

Livid.

**Friday 12th February**

Note to self. If there has to be a serious conversation had with a child, stop what you're doing, be still and face them. I learned that lesson the hard way today. We were walking down to the paddock for Forest School and two little darlings were picking twigs up and throwing them at each other to see if they could poke each other's eyes "right out". I was walking in front of them so I looked over my shoulder to tell them off, but carried on walking and ended up ploughing straight into a tree. They started laughing and I couldn't blame them. My hair was stuck on a branch, I had bark on my cheek, there were little cartoon birds flying around my head. The lesson was lost on them but to be fair, it was hilarious.

HELLO HALF TERM!

**Saturday 13th February**

I went back to see the house for a second viewing today with Mum, Dad (down for the weekend) and Di. They all love it and I am putting in an offer! Yikes!

**Sunday 14th February**

No word on the house yet. I'm driving Mum crazy wondering aloud every 5 minutes what will happen. She has the patience of a Saint, my Mum.

Also sidestepped Valentines Day. I'm not a huge fan. I always hated it at school where you could buy roses to send to people and they'd come round in your lessons to hand them out and I never got one. Maybe people bought them for themselves but I think that's just me being a bit bitter about it! Eddie seemed happy to avoid it too so we're on to a winner! He did, however, draw a photo of an old man farting himself up into the air. Why do all men find flatulence so hilarious? This is the level of romance I can expect from this relationship. This and him rubbing his butt on my head and saying "hahaha you're a butthead". I must admit, I did laugh at that one.

**Monday 15th February**

With a little bit of negotiation (mostly from Dad, the business mastermind), I've had an offer accepted! Holy moly!! I immediately started sending Mum messages about all the things I need to think about and buy, and she had to point out that she's at work and I would need to wait until she came home. I'm like a child who can't wait when an adult is talking to someone else. How dare she work when I'm not and I need to shop! As she was too busy for her youngest daughter (she was not amused when I pointed this out), I popped out for a lovely celebratory lunch with Dad; we had a pie at a gorgeous pub the Fleur de Lys and I had to have a little nap afterwards. I then went online and bought about 6 different vases with artificial flowers. Priorities.

**Tuesday 16th February**

Ah pancake day. Such joy in so much sugar! It turns out, my sister's boyfriend Maximus is a big fan of making pancakes, so Eddie and I went over to his house with Di for pancakes and it was glorious! We also discovered today that he's the male version of me and it's hilarious to see Di confused when we say the same thing at the same time! Apart from enjoying fart jokes. This he shares with

Eddie and the two of them bonded. Hard. Regardless of this, we had a really great time as a four and he is a world class pancake chef. He can stay.

**Thursday 18th February**

I've had such a great few days! Went for dinner with Di and we just laughed for about 3 hours straight, managed to catch up with a load of friends and am popping down to Somerset for the weekend to see my bestie! Good mood you say?!

(Bed time: 11pm. Probably should be later considering this is what time most normal adults go to bed on worknights)

**Saturday 20th February**

I love Axbridge. It's so cute and farmer-y and is just so peaceful. Even though my friend lives in a village it's utterly surrounded by fields and we had a little wander and got a bit lost. I'm also a bit proud of how much wine we drank last night, but also not proud at all, because I can handle it less and less as the years go by. Pansy.

**Sunday 21st February**

Bestie and I went to the pub last night with her boyfriend and his mates. They played pool and the loser has to streak round the table. I saw my best friend's boyfriend's entire butt. I don't know where we go from here. It's kept me distracted from worrying about going back to school tomorrow though I suppose!

# Chapter 4
# Spring term 2

**Monday 1st March**

PE has been going so much better since that first lesson, but there's still one thing we have not managed to figure out. Somehow, when the children get changed, their clothes go AWOL. Suddenly and recklessly, Sandeep has no shorts, Steve only has one pump, twenty of them have their shoes on the wrong feet and for some inexplicable reason Phillipa's pants have disappeared. She'll have no explanation as to why she took them off, either. It's like when you get your laundry out of the washing machine and you suddenly have three odd socks. It's absolutely guaranteed.

So, notes to myself about for PE lessons:

1. Children should get changed at a table or in a given space to ensure their clothes have limited scope to magically disperse themselves around the room.
2. When entering the hall, either give children a time limit (five seconds or so) to find a space and sit cross-legged, or give them a set amount of time to do laps of the hall to get their initial energy out before coming together for instruction.
3. Allow yourself to giggle when you say things like "hold your balls still" or "stop touching your equipment". This will always be funny and there's no shame in it. Even TTA smiles about it.
4. Have a bell or whistle or something to gather their attention that isn't your voice – sound really carries in a hall so don't let yourself get a sore throat every Monday afternoon.
5. Don some sportswear. I used to hate it for some reason, but spending the afternoon in your sweats is glorious – I must fully take advantage of this! I remember my 90 year-

old year 5 teacher at school taking us outside for PE in her kitten heels and pleated skirt. I never understood this.

6. Don't underestimate how awful their spacial awareness is. Have a first aid kit ready, be really clear about your instructions and have some ice packs on hand. Donald gets huge laughs by spinning around as quickly as he can, but this will usually result in him falling over, bumping into you or stepping on your toe. I will reflect this in his end of year grade.
7. If you do PE in the hall after lunch, it will smell terrible and there will always be a stray pea somewhere. Even if there were no peas cooked that day. Send the children on a pea hunt before getting going with the activities, but there's not much to be done about the smell.

**Tuesday 2nd March**

I've had a marvellous idea to get a class pet for my class. They could learn to take care of it, develop some extra kindness and empathy, plus it might help with some of their anxieties. Well done me, great teacher-ing! I floated the idea of a class pet to my headteacher, who thought it was a lovely idea. I don't want anything with fur, to avoid allergies, or anything that would require a complete overhaul to clean on a regular basis. I can barely keep my house clean, never mind someone else's. So today we had a little google and checked out some options.

Together, the class and I came up with some ideas. I put some of their suggestions on the list just to humour them, like ants, because, well why not? I did, however, have to veto a couple of wildly ridiculous suggestions like a horse. Come on now. We spent some time researching what each animal would need to live in, eat, how to take care of them etc. We genuinely put a lot of work into this and everyone is really invested in it. Even if we (I) changed our minds (my mind) and decided we (I) no longer wanted to keep a class pet (because I'd have to take it home in the holidays), the process provided some excellent learning opportunities for research skills.

**Wednesday 3rd March**

TTA revisited the pet idea with the children today and somehow, they arrived at a giant African land snail. Brilliant! It will be really interesting, doesn't need a lot of maintenance or a big cage, eats lots of lettuce so that's easy, no fur to enrage someone's senses, and if you wear gloves you can give them a warm bath occasionally! Weird, I know, but technically still a caring act so that's nice. So I went online tonight and found a woman whose snail has just had about fifty babies (yikes), so she's giving them away, hurray! I've ordered a tank thing and some soil and moss and a little heater (because they get chilly) so when they arrive we can get it set up and then I'll go collect two snails!

**Thursday 4th March**

World Book Day.

I remember non-uniform days at school. You put on your favourite pair of jeans and feel invincible, you strut into school feeling like you're no longer a student there because you're not wearing a uniform. Multiply that by thirty and that's the energy level you're met with at 8.45am when the children have to dress up in a costume. Don't get me wrong, it is adorable to see children come to school in either their own clothes, or party clothes, or in a costume, but I really need to start drinking coffee to make sure I have enough energy to match them. They get SO excited! Little Red Riding Hood walks through the door and can't wait to show you everything she's packed in her basket (which inevitably ended up taking up the entire space on my desk when she couldn't be bothered to carry it round any more; this happened at about 9.30am), Iron Man charges in and refuses to take their mask off, resulting in slight bumps with furniture and various muffled grunts throughout the day (no assessment opportunities here), and the gorgeous homemade costume which this child has to explain to absolutely everyone because nobody knows what character a bright green box could be. We also faced some flagrant disregard for English weather and age appropriate clothing. There were girls in shoes with small heels that they couldn't walk in, children without any jumpers or coats even though it's only 7 degrees, just because they're wearing a cape, and many, many wands that get broken, lost or shoved in places people don't want a wand shoved.

There was also always going to be at least one child who came in their school uniform. Today there were three. I really felt for these children as someone who has done this personally in the past. We told the children the day before, sent extra notes home and targeted any parents on the door at the end of the day yesterday that we thought might need an extra reminder (like me, I would need this). Yet, there were still three children in their uniform and they looked absolutely mortified. One parent managed to rush home and back again, having just forgotten the day, but for the other two, we got a couple of fun costumes out of the role play corner so that they didn't feel too left out.

The problem with a non-uniform day, is that they mostly occur when lessons are still expected to take place as normal. So you have double the amount of energy which means double the amount of behaviour management with probably half the amount of application. If you put out the paints and a cowboy goes home with purple splotches all over his brand new shirt, this probably won't go down too well with their parents. I took a class photo immediately once they were all in because I knew it won't be long before some of them have had to change into their PE pumps, Alice in Wonderland's dress would have mud all over it and Thor had lost their hammer.

**<u>Friday 5th March</u>**

The stuff for the snails arrived whilst I was at school today, so once I got home I set it all up; a tank thing, some soil in a block that you add water to and it expands (mind blown), a water dish and a heat mat. Once that was done, I popped over to a council flat in Coventry and picked two slimers up from the woman giving them away. Snails aren't cute. I'm not an idiot, however baby snails are super cute! I popped them on some lettuce in a plastic container and took them home to get them settled in. I'll take them in on Monday and introduce them to their new family. Mum is horrified that I have two snails in the house that I'm feeding and heating! She keeps threatening to throw salt on them.

**Saturday 6th March**

I've been doing lots of house stuff this week. The solicitor is absolutely rubbish and I have to keep on top of what he's doing. I've had a shirty email basically telling me to stop emailing them and when they've got owt to tell me they'll get in touch with me, to which I basically replied no because without me emailing you I don't believe owt would get done. The estate agents are fantastic though. There's one woman in particular who is so on the ball. She calls me quite often and if I've struggled with the solicitors she'll call and have a go at them too! I'm so grateful for her. We're getting a property survey done (I say we, even though it's my house, because I can't do anything without my parents as I don't know what I'm doing!) so fingers crossed for that. There's no chain though, the lady who's selling is a million years old and moving in with her son and I'm obviously a first-time buyer so hopefully it won't be too stressful. Famous last words?!

**Sunday 7th March**

Why do people iron clothes? Or perhaps the question should be, why do people buy clothes that need ironing? I tend to do the ironing for me and Mum and it's not a bad set up, we watch something terrible on a Sunday night and I iron away, but I'm mostly just doing her work uniforms because I'm trying to buy things now that can just dry hanging or flat so it's not necessary. If I came home from uni of a weekend or in the holidays, Mum and I used to watch things like Rosemary and Thyme on a Sunday night. It was awful but I still find I want that comforting routine on a Sunday night.

**Monday 8th March**

The children and the snails were introduced to each other today. We were all so excited! We held a vote on what to call them and this was an entire lesson in itself. The children were mostly suggesting their own names and couldn't understand that that might become a tad confusing if there was a human Mehmet and a snail Mehmet. Otherwise we somehow ended up with a list of adjectives, like Slimy and Glittery. I don't think they've ever had to name anything before and this should be added into the curriculum.

Welcome to Reception, Boss Baby and Suzie.

(Bed time: back to 8.45pm)

**Tuesday 9th March**

Today, we spent most of the day practising for the upcoming Mother's Day assemblies. This. Is. Adorable. We painted pictures of our Mums (as in, the children did, I didn't) and then came up with words to describe them. I was desperately trying to help the children understand how much their mums do for them and for them to be grateful. They all seem to really love their mums, but there's not enough appreciation there. I can't blame them, they're very young, but I think of my mum still taking care of me when I'm now an adult. She still cooks for me, takes care of me when I'm poorly, teaches me things, will sew holes in my coats, picks things up from the post office for me and is so so so so patient with me. She's so fantastic and I see that in a lot of these mums (not to the same extent, nobody can match my mum!) and these children just have no idea. But then I probably didn't when I was their age.

For the assembly, we learned two songs to sing and it is ADORABLE! We'd put some activities out for Mother's Day and without being asked, so many of them chose to draw their mum a picture or made them a collage or something. The great thing about being in an early years classroom is that you can make your own Mothers' Day card at work as you have lots of access to tissue paper and glitter so you never forget to buy one! There was a lot of love in our classroom today.

**Wednesday 10th March**

After school today, I had a little rearrange of the classroom. I've done this before but today it was to allow for my own specific body type. I have discovered that there is no greater dismay felt, than when you bop a child on their head with your butt as you try to get past their chair. How embarrassing.

**Thursday 11th March**

Gary has been diagnosed with diabetes. He's got to have an insulin pump. He's taking it like an absolute champ, like nothing about diabetes is going to phase him at all. His Mum came in for the morning to show me and TTA what to do and how to take care of him and I have to admit, it's really daunting. He's got a box of sweets in the classroom now and we have to keep an eye on his sugar levels and document everything he eats. This is really scary, I'm not a nurse! This is so much responsibility and I'm really nervous about it. His Mum assured me that it's not such a big task and that if he goes under or over it's easily fixed, but there's so much to think about and with Blake being a ticking time bomb every day I'm just really scared. It's a good job Gary is so ok with everything, he seems so relaxed about it, thank goodness!

**Friday 12th March**

Guess what sport relief means? You got it, non-uniform. Another non-uniform day. Another off the charts behaviour day. I'm having purely chocolate and wine for dinner.

**Saturday 13th March**

I found a guy online selling a double mattress so he brought it round in his van today. I made Mum come out with me in case he kidnapped me. Di can't quite come to stay any more because I'm slowly filling the spare rooms with stuff I'm buying prematurely for the house but I CAN'T STOP!

**Sunday 14th March**

Spent the whole day at Eddie's. I'm really behind with work but it was worth it for the smile on my face. The trouble is, as soon as I got home I got that Sunday night anxiety tummy feeling. It's so strange, I love my job but every Sunday I get nervous or whatever the feeling is. Most people I speak to say they have the same thing but it's so annoying.

**Monday 15th March**

That stupid anxiety last night really slapped me in the face today; I blame it for having to do my to-work journey twice this morning. I hadn't slept very well so ended up getting up later than I'd like and when rushing to leave the house, I had slipped my feet into two ballet pumps from the heap by the front door, only to look down as I entered the school building to realise one was pink and one was blue. Fail. Apparently it's lucky to accidently wear different shoes, but I think this is just what unfortunate people tell themselves to feel better. Like those people claiming it's good luck to be pooed on by a bird. How on earth could that be regarded as good luck? You just got poo on you. Poo! Unless the next bird flying over me is going to drop a butt-load of cash into my lap I reject this 'lucky' theory entirely. Wearing odd shoes just made me feel like an idiot. Note to self, keep spare shoes at school.

**Tuesday 16th March**

Mothers' day assembly number one. Adorable. Everything went to plan, nobody refused to do it even though so many of them were really nervous and most of the mums cried in happiness at some point. Job done.

(Bed time: 9pm. This seems to be pretty standard now)

**Wednesday 17th March**

Mothers' day assembly number two and we did not learn our lesson from the Christmas performances. We had the same set up – yesterday was in the afternoon and they went straight home with their mums if they were in the audience. Today, it was first thing in the morning and obviously they couldn't go straight home with their mums, so we had many a tear shed. We had to call Blake's mum to come and get him because his reaction was so severe there was no way we were getting him back in the classroom and it took us ages to calm some of the others down. Emotional day.

**Thursday 18th March**

Today, I had a conversation about birthday presents with a couple of children who have just celebrated the big 5. Here's how it went:
Me: "It's my birthday soon, what are you going to get me?"
Clive: "Chocolate!" (Someone's been listening to me talk about my favourite things, good work kid!)
Clarence: "Makeup!" Rude. I don't tend to wear much makeup, so I wasn't sure where this had come from. I went in for clarification
"Do you think I need more make-up?"
"Yes."
Well then, Clarence. I guess we've reached an impasse and should go our separate ways. In fairness to her, a couple of days ago I rocked up at school wearing eyeliner which I don't normally do, and TTA said to me "ooh you look lovely today! Are you wearing more makeup?" Hurtful. So perhaps I did need more makeup and I should start taking advice from five-year-olds who clearly think I could better myself.

**Friday 19th March**

On a day when you have dressed up like Winnie the Witch, you do not want to be stopping in at Tesco on the way to work to buy some lunch. This is what happened to me, however. For World Storytelling Day, the English lead decided that in addition to dressing up for World Book Day, the staff should also dress up today. The good thing, is that because the children weren't dressed up, their behaviour didn't completely deteriorate. The other good thing is that we spent most of the day engaging with story-based activities, encouraging each other to tell, read and listen to stories and I got to play my personal hero! I really identify with Winnie the Witch. She's a bit of a recluse, is incredibly clumsy and loves to do magic. If I could do magic I think I might actually be Winnie the Witch. I read loads of her stories (yes I said that like they're her autobiographies) throughout the day and by the end of it (yawns counted), lots of the children were totally enamoured with her and Wilbur too. Job done. I should be working on commission here. What a great start to my birthday weekend! I managed to leave at 4.30pm today, what an absolute joy! Hello cocktails and cake with Eddie!

**Saturday 20th March**

My birthday! I am full to the brim of cake and joy.

**Sunday 21st March**

Have I mentioned it was my birthday yesterday?! I had such a great day with Mum and Di, Dad came over too and we all went for lunch. They're so kind and thoughtful, I always feel really special on my birthday. Mum and Di had decorated the house with all the birthday balloons and banners etc. and Di even came to stay last night. It's such a treat all waking up in the same house. Dad bought me the biggest bunch of flowers, which sit smiling at me in my bedroom.

I went out in the evening to Snobs of all places (stickiest floors in the business), with a few friends and Eddie came! It's the first time we've been out together with my friends and it was awesome, he's just so much fun and they all love him. He bought me some awesome presents, which I wasn't expecting, including Batman socks that have their own capes! He gets me.

My Grandparents and Uncle came over for the day today and we had our usual wonderful family time. It's such a shame because I've genuinely had a magnificent birthday; I feel very loved and I've been spoilt rotten, but the whole time I've just been thinking oh no I'm going to be so tired for work on Monday. How do people work full time and have fun and not feel like they're a zombie the whole time?

**Monday 22nd March**

I am amazed at how cross parents are with me about the items of PE kits or uniforms that have gone missing that I am not able to find. Why am I amazed? Because when I ask "Does it have their name in it?" they say something ridiculous like "No, but it's a red jumper aged 4-5". They all are, dumbass (I only think this, I don't say it to their stupid faces). I have thirty children aged 4-5 who wear red jumpers because that's the school uniform. But you can't take 5 minutes to write your child's name in their clothes? No no, don't bother, just let me sort through all the clothes that don't have names in and I'll have a guess as to which one is your child's.

I've taken to getting TTA to help me check the children's PE kits and their jumpers or cardigans to avoid having that conversation every single week and we've even started writing children's names in their clothes! What a waste of my time.

**Tuesday 23rd March**

So. It turns out that giant African land snails are nocturnal. We didn't realise this before now. Nowhere in our research did we come across the fact that they are nocturnal animals. So that's quite a big disappointment. Quite early on in the snails being in the classroom, Jim, who has a particular interest in animals, said "why have we got a nocturnal pet? What's the point? It's asleep all day." Right well, aside from the fact that you're absolutely right, how dare you only point this out now! Where were you for the last month when we were all doing research? Hmm? Stupid snails.

**Wednesday 24th March**

There was an Easter themed lunch at school today and as staff, if we ate it with the children we got it for free! Claudio accidentally spat on my jacket potato that I was only a third of the way into. This is why I don't eat with the children at lunch time.

(Bed time: 9.30pm. This feels very late to me now)

**Thursday 25th March**

Apparently primary school teachers aren't as clever as secondary school teachers. This is a popular joke for comedians and probably secondary school teachers, but why is it a competition? Secondary school teachers have incredible knowledge on their subject, without a shadow of a doubt. They are incredible. Plus, they have to deal with a multitude of emotions and hormones and attitudes! That's amazing. Primary school teachers have to be experts in at least nine different subjects. We also have to deal with emotions plus many a bodily fluid. Why is this any less difficult or impressive? Let's not compare, let's just appreciate the individual genius of each teacher.

**Friday 26th March**

My Dad is down from Cumbria this week and came to meet me for lunch today. He was sat outside the front of the school in his car and as I walked the children out of the classroom down to the main school for lunch, I said oh look it's my Dad waiting to meet me for lunch, wave to Daddy Youngwood! So this line of 30 four-year-olds waved to my Dad, who waved back. Later, Dad said that it felt really weird to be a man, sat outside a primary school waving to a bunch of children. I hadn't considered how that might look, whoops!

It was really lovely going out of school for lunch, though. So many days I eat standing at the photocopier or in my classroom alone or I forget to eat altogether as I'm trying to get ready for the afternoon, so it felt like a proper break and I was so much more ready for the afternoon. Aside from being really sleepy from all the chips I ate, of course. I might try to remember this and make more of an effort to have a break at lunch time, even for just 15 minutes to reset.

**Saturday 27th March**

We're still a couple of weeks away from Easter, yet I've already eaten two Easter eggs and about five crème eggs. I can't decide if Easter chocolate is better than Christmas chocolate or the other way round.

Chocolate coma. Also then ate another easter egg.

**Sunday 28th March**

Mother's Day! Or Mothering Sunday, if you are my Gran and a stickler for things to be as they should be. Mum always has to scour the shops extra hard to find a card that says Happy Mothering Sunday, whereas my Mum gets insanely cross if we call her mother! Di and I made Mum breakfast...it used to be breakfast in bed, but Mum would always be up before us or desperate to get up because she's not great at lying around being lazy, so we gave up on that a couple of years back! Now it's just breakfast. Though we eat together, which is nice. It was sunny so we took it outside, though my sister gets cold really quickly, so it was a brief stint! Gran, Grandad and my uncle came over mid-morning and Di and I cooked a roast and made a fuss of Mum and Gran. I love Mother's Day. We're just all together.

We messaged Dad later on too. His mum, our Nan, died a few years ago and she was magnificent. Such a warm, caring lady who always had Softmints or similar in her bag! She made the absolute best chocolate cake and steak pie and I remember her giving up smoking and having to twirl a pen in her hand whenever she was on the phone as a replacement. She did, however, used to put the vegetables for lunch on to boil when we called to let her know we were setting off to get to her house. From Solihull. To Blackpool. Peas do not need three hours.

Dad started bringing her on holidays with us after Grandad died and I remember four main things about these holidays:

1. Good God can she snore. I sincerely hope this is not a glimpse into my future.
2. She tried a Bacardi and coke for the first time and then got pretty hooked on them!
3. She lost her hat to sea whilst out on a catamaran, but wasn't upset about it. On the contrary, she was telling everyone in the hotel about her adventure!
4. She asked the most ridiculous questions. Like me saying I'm eating a chicken burger and her response being "ooh what's in that then?"

It must be so hard to lose a parent and I never ever want to experience it. I have such wonderful female role models in my life that I love celebrating on Mother's Days.

**Monday 29th March**

Pet update. Disappointment number 2 is that giant African land snails hibernate if it gets too cold. Perfect English pet huh. Sleeps in the day and shuts up shop when it's cold. Useless. Even though we left their heater on constantly, one of the snails sealed itself up almost immediately and didn't come back out. Maybe it had stage fright being in front of the children (think Darla in Finding Nemo), or maybe it was just rude. Anyway, it's been really warm recently, one of those times when English people are so excited to talk about how hot it is, but the sealed one hasn't come back out. We pronounced it dead. The stupid snail has no life left in it and it was a tad traumatic for the children who could see that it was not going to come back out. I did not want to have to set up a pet bereavement session, so, I've done what all good liars do, and went to find a replacement.

Back to the woman with all the snail babies I went over the weekend. Back to school with a new snail atop a lettuce leaf early this morning. I picked up the dead snail to throw it into the bin, only to realise it wasn't dead at all! The little git had sensed its' impending morbidity and come out! I was livid. It must've known I was about to throw it in the bin and made a dash for freedom. Well, not a dash, snails can't dash. What's the word for a super slow, boring version of a dash? Anyway. Now we have three snails and I had to come clean to the children that I was going to replace one and that's why we have three. It turned out well in the end though, as we've been talking about Easter, Dasha pointed out that the snail came back to life "just like Jesus"!

It's Eddie's birthday but he's with his parents and brother for dinner so I'll see him later in the week, *swoon*!

**Tuesday 30th March**

We had a staff meeting last night about the format for the reports we need to write for our classes. I am terrified! Apparently they take anywhere between 1.5 and 3 hours per report. So 90 extra hours on top of our current 40-60 hours per week in the next couple of months, plus proof reading and editing time. Yikes! I'm already thinking of the gorgeous children who I'm really excited to write about, pointing out how helpful they are, willing to learn and always polite. The ones who make me laugh every day and always say good morning when they come in. The ones that talk so animatedly about their families with such love it makes my heart full.

Then I think of Jiminy and how selfish and withdrawn he is. I think of Blake who is scaring me and all the other children daily. I think of Mehmet who is spoiled and cocky and believes he's better than everyone else. How can I reword "This child is a constant drain on my energy"? I've started having a look at previously written reports to get a feel for how to word things but I want to write as much from scratch as possible for the personal comment and the core subjects. For the foundation subjects (Art etc.) it's a bit more acceptable to create a couple of different comments and then just personalise them, mostly because they've asked parents and the majority of which said they don't read those comments anyway! They're mostly interested in their grades, effort and personal comment. So that makes these upcoming hours of work seem really worth it!

A friend I've got at another school said they've changed their system so that they only write comments for a couple of them, then just provide a standard overview of what was learned for the other subjects with an effort grade. This sounds like a dream! I suggested it but it was very quickly dismissed. Maybe they'll think about it and bring it in next year, but for now it's writing everything for parents to not read!

**<u>Wednesday 31st March</u>**

With it getting towards the end of term, I am exhausted. The children are exhausted and their emotions are all over the place (I completely sympathise with them!), there are loads of little snipes and arguments over the smallest of things yet the workload isn't going anywhere. So I've started getting up later and I've been coming in later and later every day. This morning I rolled in around 8.30, which is absolutely unprecedented. To my horror, I'd forgotten that I'd agreed to meet a parent at 8.15 this morning and only remembered when I turned up to school and saw her parked on the road. I did the only thing that felt right in the moment and told her that I was sincerely sorry for being late but that I'd got stuck in traffic behind a road accident.

I'm going to hell for being a liar.

It's Mum's birthday today so Di and I took her out for dinner and we had a cocktail each, which made it feel like the weekend! My Mum is genuinely the kindest, most selfless person you'll ever meet so we like to make a fuss of her on her birthday but it never feels like enough.

**Thursday 1st April**

I'm not sure I'll ever drink on a school night again. What a silly idea. My poor head.

It was the final day of the Easter egg decorating competition today. There were some AMAZING entries! There was a batman egg, a ghost egg, a scarecrow egg and a whole farm of egg animals! Some children had painted pretty designs, there was even a Rangoli selection and they all looked incredible. Getting them home at the end of the day when children are already carrying more than they can manage sure was a challenge, and nobody looked more gutted to be taking them back home than the parents! I think they assumed we'd just keep them but what on earth would we do with 350 cooked, decorated eggs?!

(Bed time: 8.20pm... but I blame the hangover for this)

**Friday 2nd April**

I have a photograph of me from when I'm about four-years-old taking part in an Easter bonnet parade but I don't remember it at all. My Mum has always been incredible at making things from scratch (costumes etc.) so we clearly had a great time with this bonnet! I hadn't seen it done on any of placements but they do it here and it is SO CUTE! Unfortunately, idiot me had forgotten about it so after scouring all the shops after work yesterday, all I'd managed to find was a headband that has lamb ears on it, so I really let the side down with them and am determined to make a proper effort next year.

All the children came in with their beautiful hats (some of which are clearly just shop bought but I don't have any platform to judge that!) and Sandeep even had one with real chocolate eggs on! I didn't realise this at first until we were lining up ready to go to the hall and I saw him eating his hat! I really panicked until I realised there are edible elements. We went down to the hall and the site manager had put the stage up for us again and we had a little walking show in front of the parents to the song Easter Parade!

The children and I had a great time, unfortunately, TTA missed the entire thing because Blake wasn't having any of it. We'd tried to prepare him for it with visual symbols, a countdown and lots of prep for what was coming, but we started lining up and he went round ripping everyone's hats off their heads and throwing them around. It was heart-breaking. His Dad was called because he couldn't calm down, but everyone else managed to get out and have a lovely time at the Easter bonnet parade so that was a lucky distraction.

I cannot adequately describe how happy I am to have two weeks off.

**Saturday 3rd April**

Eddie offered to come over and help me take a load of stuff to the tip today. He parked up on the drive and we were in and out of the garage or through the side gate to the garden. I put all my stuff in the car and then went back into the house to close the garage up, which you can only do from the inside. I went out of the front door, which closes on a latch, and realised I hadn't unlocked the porch door yet. And all my stuff was in the car. So I was locked in the porch. Luckily, I had my phone in my pocket and I could see Eddie's

confusion when he was sat in the car looking at my name come up calling him on the phone.
Eddie – hello?
Me – hi... I'm locked in the porch...
Eddie – of course you are.

He wasn't even a little bit surprised (rude) laughed for far too long before letting me out.

**Sunday 4th April**
Back to my Grandparents' to celebrate Mum's birthday today. We popped out for lunch and had a bit of a wander round the shops, which was lovely. When we got back, of course my grandparents had already made the birthday cake ready for us to decorate. I tried to create a picture of Mum by piping icing on the top of her cake and it was not pretty; poor Mum! She was gracious as ever and said how wonderful it was...I wonder how many other times she's lied like this to our faces! I often feel guilty about how little appreciation I must show my Mum. She's utterly selfless and fun and generous and kind (all the things I'm not!), and whilst we always try to spoil her on her birthday it always makes me think that maybe I could do more outside of her birthday.

Urgh, I'm going to end up at a garden centre aren't I.

**Monday 5th April**
I went to Ashend House farm today to check it out because we're coming here for a trip on the second day of next term and I haven't been there in a really long time. I took my Mum with me and because we were doing a rekey for school, we got in free! Bonus! I had to pinpoint where we were going to eat (always my first thought when heading out for the day), the location of the toilets and get a general sense for the lay of the land. There was a new-born foal that was a day old and already up and about on its feet! I've never seen such a young horse before and we stood watching it for ages; it was just like Bambi! There were also a bunch of tiny piglets that were just so cute. It was so much fun and I am really excited to come back here. Oh, also to bring the children.

**Tuesday 6th April**
Whole day spent writing reports. My eyes are broken and my brain doesn't work anymore.

**Wednesday 7th April**
Hanging out with Eddie on the sofa.
Me – "Eddie, your nose is in my eye"
Eddie – "That's your problem, not mine"
Bellend. I guess he's not wrong though.

**Thursday 8th April**
I've had two solid days of just catching up with friends, it's been so lovely! The only problem is, we all love going out for food and drinks, and since I have more individual friends than one big group, I do this on repeat whilst catching up with them all. So along with about 6 Easter eggs that I've already had that's probably an extra stone in weight I've gained this week!!

**Friday 9th April**
I'm going skiing tomorrow so have spent the day packing (which I love) and trying on all our old thermal stuff. There's a lot that we've had for years now and it's a bit dated and gross, so I went out to panic buy some new stuff and spent a fortune, it's insane.

I started skiing when I was in primary school; Dad took me and Di to Killington and I remember it being so icy and there not being a whole lot of snow to ski on. Di and I both went into morning ski school, then skied with Dad in the afternoon. Di has always picked things up quicker than me and also tries harder than me, so she got moved up to the next level of ski school after a couple of days and I got left in the beginner one. I love Di so much but being left while she got better felt rubbish and I've always struggled with resilience and not being as good at anything as she is, so one day when I fell over I made it out to be worse than it was so that I could skip skiing. I had to go sit inside with someone who worked in the ski school and we played card games all morning. When we got home, I refused to go on any more skiing holidays for a couple of years because I just hated everything about it.

A while later, somehow I agreed to try it again and I'm so glad I did because I absolutely love it! I know that Di is glad I'm back too, we like to do these things together as we've always been a support to each other growing up with divorced parents. I went on a ski trip without her once (I can't remember why) and it wasn't the same without her at all, I think I asked to go home on the second day!

I'm pretty good at skiing now, though I'm mostly a fair weather skier. I'm not into it when it's hard work, like when it's really slushy or icy or when it's so cloudy that you can't see where you're going because everything around you is the same shade of white. I love it first thing in the morning where the piste bashers have been out and the snow is like corduroy and the slopes are steep so you can just whiz down! I'm so excited.

**Saturday 10th April**

We're going skiing today! Just popping casually over to France for a week with Dad's friends Mel and Ronnie. They're such great fun, we've often been away on skiing holidays with them. In the past they've brought their kids too but none of them could come this time.

We got the train to London, where we met Mel and Ronnie, then we went to get on the Eurostar. Dad and Mel are hilarious; they're very gentlemanly and offer to carry the skis and poles because they're heavy and awkward, but they're both not so great with spatial awareness and we had to walk around them to help them avoid shattering people's noses as they turned corners. It's such a faff to get all your skiing stuff to where you're going; we've talked before about just hiring them while we're out there but we never seem to get round to selling our own stuff.

We just need to get the sleeper train now and tomorrow, we will wake up in snowy France! I'm trying to not be the girl on her phone the whole time but I really miss Eddie. One of the best things about him is that we always want to tell each other everything, even tiny silly details about our day we want to share with each other, so I'm trying to message him covertly so that I can still talk to him but not annoy everyone!

**Sunday 11th April**

Sleeping on a train, albeit one that has beds, is not the best night's sleep you'll ever have. They're weird compartments that have two bunk beds, but the top beds fold up against the wall so that before you go to sleep you can sit on the bottom beds like sofas. The three of us plus Mel and Ronnie had dinner and drinks in our compartment and played some ridiculous games, then Mel and Ronnie went off to their compartment for the night. I kept getting disturbed throughout the night, but waking up at silly o'clock this morning in France and leaving the train to see snow everywhere was just magical. We had a minibus come and pick us up to take us to the chalet where we'll be staying. Di and I will share a room, which I love because we can be so silly together and debrief about each day, and then there's a communal kitchen, dining area and lounge with a wood burning fireplace. We have an amazing chalet host called Freddie who will make us breakfasts and dinners, plus afternoon tea, which is just my favourite part of skiing! We tend to finish up about 3pm, so then you get back to the chalet to shower and change and there's a different cake there for you every day.

One of mine and Eddie's mates was a chalet host back in the day and it sounds like an amazing job! You're up early and working late, cooking and cleaning the chalet, but you get the whole day to ski or snowboard and one day off a week to sleep or party. It sounds great!

Once we'd ditched our stuff at the chalet we went straight out for a quick run on the slopes. It wasn't the most successful first outing we've ever had! Di and I got on a chairlift and popped off up the mountain and Dad, Mel and Ronnie got on the one behind us. When we got to the top, however, only Dad and Ronnie got off... It turns out, that when they had all sat down on the chair, Ronnie had put her hands down, meaning Mel sat on one of them. Once it had moved on a little bit but before they'd managed to put the safety bar and foot rest down, Ronnie had jerked her hand up to get it out from underneath Mel, but instead of sliding it out she had lifted it (and Mel with it) up, causing Mel to land face first, spread eagled in the snow below the lift!! Apparently there was a huge ordeal with the lift operator not bothering to stop the lift, but instead yelling at Mel in French and trying to drag him by a ski out of the way of the next chair that was heading up! Di and I were absolutely gutted to have missed it, but Mel is not ready to laugh about it yet so perhaps we'll hear him tell the story later in the week...

The first run of a holiday is always a little bit daunting. It's uncomfortable getting the boots on and not having much range of motion and you never know if you're going to be able to remember how to ski or not! But once you find a groove it's so freeing and the views are spectacular. As a group we don't tend to go in for awful runs like moguls or anything to narrow, but there was a point a few years ago where Dad realised that I'm now faster than him and I like to remind him of that ever year now. Mel and Dad are amazing skiers and tend to go off by themselves for a run or two every day so that they can ski harder and faster than they do with us. They can ski backwards and everything! I would say it's something to aspire to but I don't think I'll bother, I'd quite like to start doing little jumps though.

**Monday 12th April**

Every year, Dad tells me and Di to do some leg exercises before we go skiing to strengthen our muscles and I never bother, what does he know? Turns out, a lot. Good God do my thighs hurt. I hate it when he's right.

In other news, I forget that coming skiing we're at a higher-than-normal altitude. I opened the tooth paste last night and it gushed out at top speed and we lost half of it. Di and I were crying laughing. Dad loves to blame everything on the altitude whenever we come skiing. If he forgets something it's the altitude, if he falls over skiing it's the altitude, if he drops his pole, it's the altitude! It always makes us giggle and the joke never gets old.

I've been sending photos and videos to Eddie and trying to convince him that someday he might want to come with us...fingers crossed! He was a skater though so I wonder if he'd snowboard rather than ski...so he's the enemy... We also went to rival secondary schools but I can forgive all of these things because he's pretty great. Also, he told me that he got trapped in a corridor at work today! You need your ID card to get into all the different offices in his building, a bit like how lots of schools are, and he walked out of his office without his pass so couldn't get back in the office or get anywhere else! This evens us out for me getting locked in the porch and I shall now be calling him Captain Corridors (after the Mighty Boosh version, Captain Cabinets).

(Bed time: 10pm. Skiing is not a holiday that comes complete with lie-ins)

**Tuesday 13th April**

Dad has been on form today! Not for skiing but for comedy. At one point this morning when it was a little cloudy, we saw him up ahead of us totally stationary but in the skiing position, hunched over with poles up under his arms. We slowed down as we went past him and asked what he was doing, to which he replied 'skiing'. We stopped in front of him and pointed out that he wasn't moving at all and when he looked up and saw people speeding past him I think Di and I could have fallen over laughing.

Then, later in the day, the three of us were skiing together, when suddenly Dad spun around and was skiing backwards facing us. We were so impressed, but it turns out he had no intention of doing it and was so surprised by his impromptu pirouette that he couldn't figure out how to get back round again for ages!

When we got back to the chalet, we got the fire going and were settling in with our afternoon cake (lemon drizzle today mmmm). Dad asked Di to put another log on the fire and she chose quite a large one. She somehow got a bit of momentum up and launched it, sending it through the back of the fire, shattering the glass panel in the process! We laughed hard and she didn't move for a good thirty seconds in shock!

This is already a hilarious week and for once, it's not because I'm being an idiot! I love my family.

**Wednesday 14th April**

We were skiing in a white out this morning and it's so difficult to see where the piste ends and the sky begins. There are poles and trees as markers in lots of places, but not everywhere. Di and I skied down to where Mel and Ronnie were waiting and carried on. Ronnie asked us "are you not going to wait for your Dad?", so we asked where he was, unaware that he wasn't just in front of us somewhere as he normally would be leading, and she pointed and said "down there". As it turned out, Dad was in a ravine. Skis up in the air. Flat on his back like a turtle trying to get up.

My first question – "Dad are you alright?"

My second question once he'd replied yes – "Stay there so I can get a photo!" He wasn't happy about this, especially after managing to disentangle his skis and I just asked him to put them back because it would make a funnier picture. I defy anyone to truthfully say that they wouldn't have done the same thing! It took him ages to make his way out because the snow was so deep and soft that every time he took a step, his entire leg would disappear! Di had to pull him out by him grabbing on to one of her poles and I struggled to get decent photos through my laughter; I don't think I've ever laughed so much.

Because it was snowing so heavily, we decided to call it quits at lunch time and instead just had a lovely wander round the town. I don't want to break my not-falling-over streak and we can't risk losing Dad off a precipice.

**Thursday 15th April**

It was still snowing really heavily today and was due to stop mid-morning, so we decided to go sledging first thing instead and ski later on. Skiing is not so much fun when you can't see where you're skiing (and you nearly lose your Dad down a ravine), whereas lower down where the chalet was, the visibility was much better. The snow was still really deep, though, and Dad made a huge show of jumping on to his sledge, but instead ended up just disappearing straight down under the snow! He came up a good twenty seconds later about a meter down from where he had disappeared, with a head's worth of snow on top of his hat! Luckily we managed to film it so I'll be sending that off to You've Been Framed as soon as we get home. I always remember this of my Dad, just having fun and being able to be childish whatever age he is.

The afternoon was great, it did stop snowing so visibility was much better, but because it was all thick powder it isn't great for bombing it down fast, so we just played about, skiing through the trees and making slalom poles out of ourselves for the others to ski through. It was so much fun. My favourite part of any ski run, though, is that Di and I always tap our poles together like a 'cheers' before we set off. I don't know why we do it, how/when it started or why it means so much to me, but we do and it does.

I've been trying to figure out how other people look so stylish on the slopes and I don't. I think it's because I get so cold, I have my hair shoved up in plaits under my hat and then some sort of bandana or scarf round my neck that I pull up over my chin and then I get two little wind burns along my cheeks! Other people don't seem to need all of that stuff, or go red when they're cold, or get sweaty when they go inside for lunch. I think I just need to accept that I am not a good looking skier!

**Friday 16th April**

Dad's birthday is tomorrow but we'll be travelling all day, so we did lots of celebrating today instead. The chalet host made another insane breakfast and we came home to a carrot cake for our afternoon tea – Dad's favourite. We had a less eventful day of skiing today, with nobody falling over or getting lost; we just explored some different runs and had some races. We had a delicious meal in the chalet and then we went out for a drink in the evening. Dad asked for 'the local' drink, and we watched in disbelief as the bartender went along every single spirit optic on the shelf and then topped the inch of remaining space up with coke. Dad isn't a big drinker, so it was hilarious to watch him stand up after drinking this and have to hang on to the partition next to him! On the way home, we had to go up the tiniest snowy slope, and it took Dad about 15 minutes! The rest of us were literally on the floor laughing. I'm glad we got to have a fun day that he deserves for his birthday, even though it's not technically until tomorrow.

**Saturday 17th April**

Travelling all day. Tired. Miss the slopes. Don't want to go back to work. Bleurgh.

**Sunday 18th April**

We recently managed to go skiing for my 21st birthday and on the day, Dad and Di made me a birthday breakfast baguette with candles in the top and attached balloons to my coat that I had to ski with all day. I lived in fear all day of getting on and off the ski lifts and whether I'd somehow get garrotted by the balloon strings, but it turned out fine and I even got lots of strangers singing happy birthday to me in the queues for the lifts! Dad's birthday, unfortunately, fell on the changeover day, so there was no skiing at all for him, never mind attached to balloons, though with his track record this week of falling over I'm not sure balloons would have been safe to attach to him…or perhaps the would have helped to keep him upright? Either way, it's been an amazing week and I feel so lucky.

The journey home was as busy and tiring as the journey out and I have mostly chilled out all day today with Eddie; it's been so good to see him again, though I've had that horrible Sunday night feeling since about 3pm. It's so difficult to go back to work after a holiday, even though I love what I do I still get so nervous about going back.

# Chapter 5
# Summer term 1

**Monday 19th April**

I came to school today absolutely dreading it (for no logical reason) so I tried to focus on the amazing jaunt to Ashend House Farm that Mum and I had done in the holidays that I would be replicating with the children this week and that helped to make me smile. Then I had to do a risk assessment for said trip. Have you any idea how many ways there are for children to get hurt, maimed or killed on a farm? So many! Even though I'd sent a letter out just before the Easter holidays to get everything sorted, I had at least five different parents asking me really basic questions about the trip. Really? You didn't even bother to read the letter? Don't worry, I have all the time in the world, I'll just repeat the information seventeen individual times. Infuriating. I set about getting everything together after school ready for tomorrow; first aid kit, high vis jackets, sick bags, spare clothes, and then I started to have another little worry about everything that could go wrong.

Why am I even considering taking thirty children, who are not related to me, into a public space or building? This is a lot of responsibility. Especially when you're a twenty-two-year-old, fresh out of university, with lots of experience with children but have none of your own. What if I lose someone else's child? What if I accidentally achieve a Home Alone counting fail and leave someone at the farm? What if someone gets eaten by a goat? Some parents might have been glad of this but it's not really the point. I'm sure it'll be lots of fun but I sure am glad TTA is coming with me. Luckily we have Blake's Mum coming to be 1:1 with him so that's one source of comfort about how he'll react to different points throughout the day.

Wish me luck.

**Tuesday 20th April**
Ok. Trips are simultaneously the best and worst things you can do as a teacher. I remember planning this out in September and thinking that a trip to the farm for our topic 'On the Farm' couldn't be more perfect. Fun fun fun right?

That genuine worry about all the things that could go wrong that had hit me yesterday hung around and didn't leave me until all thirty children had gone home safely with their family member at the end of the day. How on earth I expected to educate them over their excitement whilst I noted their eyes darting to all the places they instinctively wanted to run to, and bringing them home in one piece is beyond me. We did it though! We all made it back and nobody got headbutted by a boar! Victory!

I tell you what, it sure was a diverse bunch of parents that got their names pulled out of the hat to come with us! There were a few parents who were magnificent helpers and really did make my life a lot easier. They had a handle on their group at all times, kept me updated with headcounts and were genuinely attentive to the children in their group, asking them educational questions and encouraging them to not be terrified of the gammy looking goose pecking its way towards them. Then. Then there were the not-so helpful ones. They were clearly only there for a free day out with their child and had no control at all! They let their child play on the swings even when I said not to, they carried all of their child's things for them even though I explicitly instructed the children to be responsible for their own coat and bag, and one parent repeatedly took photographs using their phone and I had to keep checking it was just of their child! Thank you, bellends, for being extra children to take care of today. Urgh.

However, we did have a really great time. There was that foal that was now a couple of weeks old that I was so excited to show them, but the children moved on from this very quickly and didn't seem to understand the gravity of it being so new and being able to walk already, but I had a marvellous time watching it Bambi around the yard. Plus, there was no marking for the day – glorious! No assemblies – spiffing! I wore jeans to work – are you kidding me! I'm trying to take pleasure in the small things, because I am absolutely exhausted. There are still a million photographs and observations to add to their learning journeys but this must wait until tomorrow.

(Bed time: 7.45pm. A new low)

**Wednesday 21st April**

I've reflected upon yesterday's trip and have come up with a little cheat sheet for myself.

Here's what will definitely happen, at least once, on a meticulously planned trip:

- Someone will be sick on the coach. One child minimum. Both ways.
- Most children will ask you every ten minutes from 9o'clock in the morning whether they can eat their lunch yet.
- A couple of parents will realise how truly difficult and exhausting it is being a teacher and will leave the day in awe of you and your kind. It won't be the entire selection of parent helpers, but you can be grateful for those few.
- Something will take longer than you expect (a tour, a duck ate another duck, an unruly gang of geese block your path etc.)

- A child will bring money, even though you told them not to, and will try to buy the entire gift shop for 50p.
- Someone will fall asleep on the coach on the way back to school. This is adorable and always warrants a photograph, though nobody will know why or what to do with said photograph afterwards.
- However excited about the new-born foal you are at the farm (or something similar), the children won't care, and it will personally offend you.
- It doesn't matter how exciting your trip is, how much research you put into it or how much organising it took, children will only remember and/or care about their lunch and the play area.

**Thursday 22nd April**

Frances asked me this morning when we are going on our next trip. They seemed to be under the impression that these are going to be a regular thing. I still haven't recovered from the exhaustion of this one!

I thought I would set myself some reminders for whenever that next time comes around, though.

- You can never take too many sick bags, gloves and spare clothes.
- Put the children who are likely to try to kill a chicken in your group. If there is more than one and you have a TA, try to equally portion these children out. You have the whole class and many extra adults to oversee and Gerald putting stones in people's shoes can be someone else's responsibility for the day.
- Be flexible and allow extra time for simple tasks. You might have everything planned down to the minute, but for some reason children cannot walk at a normal speed to or from the coach. The day is then already ten minutes delayed.
- Tell children where to sit on the coach! Don't leave it up to them. Set up buddy systems before leaving the classroom but then make sure to allocate them their seats, before

Katerina decides she actually wants to sit with Sandeep and then Imran cries over her friend's cruel betrayal and the start to the day is delayed another ten minutes.

- Go to the place beforehand so you know where the toilets are. I cannot stress how crucial this is.
- Don't go at the beginning of the week, because you will be Friday-exhausted by Wednesday!

**Friday 23rd April**

Why won't they leave me alone?

**Sunday 25th April**

I've spent the weekend in Edinburgh with Eddie! He's half Scottish...though I'm not sure that's why we decided on Edinburgh! It's such a beautiful city. We went up to the castle and nearly got blown over because the wind was so strong! We also went on the Royal Yacht Britannia and did an audio tour. I thought he was going to make fun of me for loving an audio tour but turns out he likes them too! Neither of us can really be bothered to read information boards in these kinds of places, but if someone is telling me things I'm all in. It was insane, I love the royal family (I think because it is deep rooted in my romantic Disney ideals of what being a royal looks like) but I got a bit annoyed at things like the staff having to basically blend into the walls in silence if a royal walks past them. This seems a bit much nowadays, surely you can come down to earth long enough to smile at someone who's working for you?

The Scottish people are generally lovely, but there have been a couple with really thick accents who have scared the crap out of me. Eddie assured me that they weren't cross or hating me, that it was just their accent, but it was scary at times nonetheless.

It's been such an amazing weekend to just hang out the two of us. Though we went into a fudge shop and bought a load, then somehow left it in the hotel room when we left to come home. Devastating.

**Monday 26th April**

Imran was following me around for ages this morning looking really sad. I kept asking if she was alright and she kept saying yes. I asked her if anything was wrong, if she wanted to play something, if she was thinking anything, if she was worried about anything; nothing. She just wouldn't leave me side. The trouble was, there was a horrendous smell in the classroom that I couldn't quite figure out. Turns out, that smell was Imran. She was super poorly but didn't want to tell me. Which meant that for that chunk of time that she was following me round, she was walking and sitting in her own, very poorly, faeces. So then we had to clean the hell out of everything that she had been in contact with and although I was mostly really sad that she was poorly but couldn't verbalise it, I was also very glad that she didn't sit on my lap. A further case for having a change of clothes in the cupboard at all times, just in case.

I can still smell that smell.

**Tuesday 27th April**

With this being the summer term, we're starting to do some transition activities for our Reception children to help them prepare for Year 1. The first thing, is that they are no longer having a separate playground for their break time. This also, and more importantly, means that I now have to do playground duty once a week with my class, Year 1 and Year 2. I've taken from the staff room that no teacher wants to do playground duty. Even in the summer, when's it's warm and sunny. I've been battling the argument in my head of praying for it to rain, but then not wanting the children to not get a break. Because then I don't get a break. And neither does their energy.

Here are some reasons why teachers hate playground duty that I have experienced just in the last week;

1. Byron will eat mud. Byron always tries to eat mud as he does not understand that the mud kitchen is fictional.
2. Isadora will tell you jokes for the entire playtime. Some of these are indeed hilarious, but the relentless telling of jokes

for hours on end whilst you're trying to break up the football arguments is tiresome.

3. Homer will sit on the friendship bench and reject any offers of play or companionship from others. He's waiting for Batman.
4. Edgar will want you to race him. Constantly. Edgar is extra-strength slow, so not only do you have to run in your boots or sandals, but you have to fake being slow also so that you're not hammering his self-confidence.
5. You fight tooth and nail to let the children play football because if they don't, they'll kick stones or sticks or their jumpers. So you give them a ball and then spend your whole break duty either refereeing or being terrified of being hit in the head after a rogue kick.
6. Gertrude and Erminia will perform show after show for you. They refuse to practise elsewhere to ensure they are in sync with each other, so you get run after run of one leading and the other trying to keep up.
7. Kipling will scrape their knee ever so slightly and will subsequently have to hold their shorts above said knee for the rest of the day, proving that they can't possibly sit on the floor, maybe for the rest of the week. They must also limp.
8. There'll be a party going on in the toilets. Everyone loves to be in the toilets at play time, especially if it's wet or cold or both.
9. Perry will throw sticks at anyone and everyone. Including you if you tell them to stop.
10. At least ten children will ignore the bell to signal they stand still at the end of playtime. Always the same ones. They think they are above the law.

**Wednesday 28th April**

The worst has happened. Isadora hugged me round the middle while I was standing up and gasped "have you got a baby in your tummy?" No. No I do not. That's the pie and mash I had last night. Mortified.

**Thursday 29th April**

What the hell Thursday? It hasn't rained, it's not particularly windy, yet we had three bumped heads, three pretty decent bloody scrapes, a vomiter, a bent-back finger and a high temperature. This class is falling apart!

(Bed time: 9pm. Is this even news anymore?)

**Friday 30th April**

May will signify the start of Year 2 SATs. The teachers are really freaking out. It's not as big a deal as it is in Year 6, but trying to get that across to the parents is apparently really tricky. They've had a few meetings with them to tell them to not panic and that they just inform part of the teacher's judgements and that they tell the children they're activity booklets. They're not strictly timed and the teachers have done a couple of practises this year, but the papers still have to be locked away and signed in and out of the main office cupboard. The parents are apparently not taking on board the idea that it's not their final assessment and there's been lots of pressure and some of the children are already really stressed. They are 6 and 7 years old. This is madness. How much learning time are they losing by doing all these tests? What does it really tell us? Some children will love the 'activity booklets' but lots of them are already really panicking and it just seems counterproductive to me. It must be even worse for the Year 6s.

**Saturday 1st May**

I'd arranged with the estate agent to go back to the (my!) house today to do some measuring up considering I'll be moving in soon. We've already checked the big things like the sofas will fit in, so today was more about things like curtains. I've got all my colour schemes worked out so just needed to know how big to get the curtains, then Mum and I went off to buy some. I've got some gorgeous satin purple ones for my bedroom and some heavy chenille red ones for the lounge. Even though I don't have a bed for the spare bedroom yet, I managed to buy some curtains and matching bedding in a duck egg blue for the spare room. I already love having my own house and I'm not even in it yet!

**Sunday 2nd May**

Went for a BBQ over at Eddie's and did pretty well to chat with people despite my social anxiety. It's quite intimidating as he is part of such a huge group, and there seem to be lots of sub groups within it; band mates, school mates, friends of friends... then there are the girlfriends. All of them are absolutely lovely, but I get a sense from some of them that there are some cliques and some smiling to your face but not behind your back sort of dealings. Luckily, since I know a few people already either through family friends or through Di, I can often avoid the politics and just hang out with people who want to eat and drink and be merry! I've got no time for high school pettiness. I had one girl tell me that when she and her husband got married, Eddie accidently stepped on her dress and left a shoeprint, so if we ever got married she'd be doing the same to me! Thank you for the warning of intentional vandalism, consider yourself off the list!

In other news, sometimes when Eddie drinks from a can one of his moustache hairs gets caught in the ring pull and as he pulls the can away it makes a really satisfying 'twang'. Apparently I'm insensitive for laughing at his pain, but it sounds hilarious.

**Monday 3rd May**

FOUR DAY WEEK! Loving a bank holiday Monday, well done England!

**Tuesday 4th May**

It's deaf awareness week so we're learning sign2sing. It's a Take That song, which is just awful, but the biggest fun is trying to get children to sing in time to a song and also sign along to a song. This is multitasking on a new level! We tried it in assembly this morning and all the staff were in hysterics. We are not a coordinated group.

**Wednesday 5th May**

Clarence's Mum asked me to help Clarence to stop having a dummy at night. This cannot fall under the remit of my job.

**Thursday 6th May**

Class photos! Thank goodness I washed my hair this morning because I'd completely forgotten about this. My first class photo felt really special. Blake refused to be in it and trashed most of the Key Stage 1 corridor in protest, but the deputy came to try to calm him down to be a different face so TTA and I were still able to be in the photograph. The children dealt with it really well, it's quite a lot of faffing and waiting for them while everyone gets into place. Jonah spent most of the time facing the back so we had to keep turning him round, Darpan had the cutest, biggest grin on his face from start to finish (this kid could work a red carpet no problem) and Musaaleh needed a safety pin to keep his trousers up...sometimes I feel like he was intentionally slipping them down! Dasha kept chanting her own name like she was competing for something and Clive could not keep his finger out of his nose, like he was desperately trying to reach his brain. But all in all, they were great and sweet and I'm so excited for my first class photo!

**Friday 7th May**

I've discovered that playing I Spy is a really great Phonics game, where you get children to identify something based on its' colour, initial sound, rhyming pattern etc. Hours of fun and it doesn't take any prep time at all! Apparently when I was young, I used to say any random letter, my family would guess for ages, and then my answer was always pram. So there you have it, nobody is born a genius. There are, however, some unfortunate errors.

Me – "I spy with my little eye, something that rhymes with dink!"
Darpan – "cock!"

Thank goodness I wasn't being observed.

**Sunday 9th May**

Spent the weekend up in Cumbria at Dad's. He told a ridiculous story about his farmer neighbour, Jack. A couple of months ago, Jack had appeared at Dad's front door:
Jack – "have you got a freezer?"
Dad – "urm yes?!"
Jack – "is it big?"
Dad – "it's big enough... why?"
Jack – "will it fit a pig?"

It turns out that a while back, Jack had got a whole pig for his daughter's wedding, which they are going to spit roast, except the wedding wasn't for a couple of months so he had to freeze the pig whole. Dad has a standing fridge freezer so it wouldn't fit in there, whereas Jack has a chest freezer. So Dad had helped Jack to empty some stuff out of the chest freezer in order to get this pig in. It was pretty tight but they managed to wedge it in. Unfortunately, Jack had not checked on said pig until Thursday when he had needed to get it out to start thawing it, only to realise that it had frozen into the chest freezer and it wasn't budging. So he'd called on Dad to help him and they ended up having to saw bits off it just to get it out!

I love the countryside.

**Monday 10th May**

We're failing children. We're failing ourselves. When asked what they want to be when they grow up, about a quarter of the class said 'a Youtuber'. This is not a real job! I say this, there are now YouTube stars on Strictly Come Dancing every year so perhaps I've gone into the wrong job after all. I'd love to be on Strictly, and they can make so much money as an influencer, but it just doesn't seem like the kind of aspiration young children should have. It feels like a copout. But then, those who want to be actresses or singers are just dreaming a lovely dream so I'm not sure why this feels different. I managed to refrain from telling them they needed a more realistic aspiration where they could contribute more to society! How old am I.

It's Ambition Week. A whole week of nurturing children's ambitions and encouraging them to aspire to great things. I absolutely love the premise of this week and I'm so excited to have loads of guests in to talk to the children about their jobs.

This afternoon, we had a Mum of a Year 1 child in who's a photographer. She's so lovely and the photos she takes are amazing. I'm not sure the children really understood that it's a job but it was good to get them thinking about something other than jobs being about the police and nursing. Speaking of which, we have a police pair and a couple of nurses coming in tomorrow!

**Tuesday 11th May**

Handcuffs suck. It might sound stupid but they really hurt! We had two police officers in this morning and I was so happy to see a man and a woman, as most of the children still think that you have to be a man to be in the police force. So that was awesome. The kids had so many questions for them (some were really disturbing, you can tell the ones who play videogames that are too old for them) and then they showed them all of their gear. The radio, the baton, the torch and then they brought out the cuffs. The woman asked the children if they thought I should be put into cuffs and every single one of them said yes! Rude. But hey I'm game, and it was awful. They didn't even tighten them particularly but they're so uncomfortable. I tried to get this across to the children (crime doesn't pay and all that) but they found it too hysterical that I was getting locked up. I'm not sure this talk had a great impact on them avoiding a life of crime but perhaps they now all want to cuff people! Better that nothing I suppose.

I thought we were having nurses in today but it turned out to be two paramedics complete with ambulance! It was awesome! They took the children out and strapped some into the 'bed', showed them loads of the stuff they have with them in the ambulance and showed them some things they might do, like bandage people or take their blood pressure. At times, I forgot that I should be teaching and got carried away with exploring for myself! They got a bit silly towards the end when they put the siren on so we had to have a little calm down time before getting ready to go home! I can't blame them though, it's been so interesting to find out about people's jobs. The paramedics also kept it quiet from the children how many people they deal with are just drunk idiots. Smart.

**Wednesday 12th May**

Fire fighters are not fit. You know when you see a film and there are fire fighters? They're always gorgeous. Ripped and toned, the women are naturally beautiful, the men send you into cardiac arrest just by smiling at you. Not in real life, my friend. No offence to the wonderful, selfless men we had turn up today, but no thank you. The women in the school (including me) did themselves (and women everywhere) a disservice by getting all squealy about the firefighters arriving this morning but we were all very disappointed at the aged, pot-bellied fire fighters in front of us.

I popped into the hall as my class were all filing in to have a chat with said firefighters first before going out to see the fire engine, but as soon as they said hi their radio went off and they had to rush off to deal with a fire. I know that had to be their priority and they went off to literally save lives, but we were all really gutted and I didn't have anything else planned! I was so grateful to be able to just nip back off to PPA so that I didn't have to think on my feet, (lazy) but they did a bit of research into firefighting and some related activities involving role play, Lego fire engines and pictures of them dressed as firefighters. Not an altogether lost day but not our finest!

**Thursday 13th May**

Today's poor lady will forever be known as the animal lady. I still don't know her name. She's just the animal lady. I can't even remember where she works...I'm assuming a zoo or a pet shop or something. My head hasn't been in it today. I'm tired and struggling a bit with keeping up with everything and still trying to keep my energy up all the time. Anyway, the lovely animal lady showed us all the animals that horrify me (tarantulas, stick insects, snakes etc.) and the children had a pretty good time. I don't think they particularly saw it as a job, apart from Jim who already loved animals, but they had a nice time and that's what counts I suppose! Not in the mood for writing today, will just leave it there.

**Friday 14th May**

The firefighters came back! This time two women, again fantastic for subverting the children's expectations and to be fair, they were much more attractive than the two men that came on Wednesday! We all got to sit in the fire engine and they turned the sirens and lights on and I was amazed at how much stuff they've got in the fire engine; there are little cubby holes everywhere! I think it really excited the children about being firefighters, especially after them having to rush off the other day.

It's been such a fun week but I'm still shattered. Their behaviour has been more challenging because we've been out of routine and Blake has had to go home early almost every single day because of some sort of crisis. I had a parent come to me after school and say how scared and cross they are that their child is around this, and whilst I'm trying so hard to understand him and find a way to help him, I totally understand where this parent is coming from. I'm constantly on edge trying to anticipate any impending freak outs and putting myself between him and the other children so that nobody gets hurt, but I'm not always quick enough and there are so many other children to work with, I can't always be there. I'm really struggling and I keep asking for help but they don't seem to keen to do anything, they just keep asking me to keep a log of everything that happens. That might be helpful in the long term but it's not easing my rising anxiety. I'm waking up in the middle of the night worried and it's getting harder to come into school every morning wondering if I'm going to be slapped or kicked or if I'll miss him throwing a chair and knocking someone out. I don't know what to do. I'm more thankful than ever for the weekend.

**Saturday 15th May**

I didn't sleep so well last night and have spent the day feeling really low. Eddie was glorious and helped to cheer me up, but it's so difficult to let go of the Blake incidents and switch off.

**Sunday 16th May**

I could not want to go to work tomorrow any less than I do right now. On top of that, I spent most of the day writing reports. Not the best weekend I've ever had.

**Monday 17th May**

These bastard snails are the worst. They've grown up so they're not cute anymore, if you don't make sure the kids clean the old food out properly you end up with awful little fruit flies everywhere, and the snails slime everything up into a super gross Ghost Busters-esque explosion. Urgh. The children have totally lost interest in them (funny that, considering they do NOTHING all day) so I've been trying to think up ways to get them more involved. Snail race? I'll keep thinking.

(Bed time: 10pm! This almost seems respectable)

**Tuesday 18th May**

Blake had an almighty meltdown today because he made a mistake in a word he was writing. Failure is clearly a big trigger. It's so awful seeing this child not able to cope and also seeing my own emotions mirrored there. I don't cope very well with feeling like a failure, but it's so hard to change that thought process. He ended up punching Jim in the back of the head before I could get to him and then gave me a really well-placed punch to a kidney. He could probably make a lot of money as a cage fighter or assassin when he's older. We had to evacuate the other children, again, and the deputy came through to help me. We tried distraction, we tried calming, we tried everything we could think of but in the end we had to restrain him. It's the all time worst feeling. He ended up just sobbing when his Mum came to collect him. They left and I turned back round to my destroyed classroom and once again, just burst into tears. My heart was going a million miles an hour. I feel so guilty that I hadn't managed to protect Jim, I'm covered in bruises and scratches and I had to work so fast to get the classroom back to normal before the other children could come back in so that they didn't see it. Rough day. It was decided that he have a couple of days at home before coming back in and I'm ashamed to say the relief I feel is immense.

**Wednesday 19th May**

A slightly worrying conversation with Phillipa today. We were drawing and chatting and I asked her what she'd drawn, she told me it was her locked in the attic at home. So I asked why she felt like drawing that and she said it's what happens when she's naughty at home; her Mum locks her in the attic. I started to have a little panic and tried to remember my safeguarding training – don't ask leading questions, don't promise to keep it a secret, remember and write down what is said word for word and pass it straight on to the Designated Safeguarding Lead. So I repeated back what she said to me "you said your mum locks you in the attic when you're naughty?" She said "yeah, it happens a lot, once I hurt my ribs falling off the roof because I'd climbed out of the attic window because I got hungry." She then saw her friend in the water area and went running over to join her. So I wrote everything down, told TTA I needed to see the headteacher urgently and went to explain what had happened.

Now, Phillipa has been known to exaggerate things before. She once told me she had 8 brothers and sisters but she just has one younger sister. She likes attention, but this was a scary admission and needed to be taken seriously. The head said she'd call mum and talk it through and then keep an eye on the situation, but that she knew the family and it seemed unlikely. There's nothing concerning about Phillipa, never any bruises, she brings a healthy packed lunch every day, she's always clean and well-dressed and presents as a happy child. I felt a bit uneasy about it in the evening but I'm glad that it's been passed on and we can monitor it all.

**Thursday 20th May**

I went on a reading course today, which was a lovely change of pace; I had an entire extra hour in bed this morning! It was held in a hotel conference room so there was lovely air conditioning and there were fancy sweets on the tables with water jugs with different fruit slices in each one. There was then a separate room for the break with the biggest variety of biscuits in that I have ever seen! Lunch, was a huge buffet and the whole thing was just amazing! I got there just before 9 and left about 3, so for the first time ever I did the hours that everyone thinks I always work and let me tell you, it was glorious. I missed the children but it was quite nice to go home without snot and playdough and paint all over me and there was nothing extra to do once it had finished. I feel so relaxed! (Oh, also the course was pretty interesting.)

**Friday 21st May**

Well, today did not start how I had thought it would. I felt really positive after having a little break yesterday and came back into school full of information from the course to tell everyone about. As soon as I got to school, the headteacher called me into her office. This is not fun! I've met with her several times but it's always scary, like I'm a child again being called in to be told off! It's always been fine but this time it was not. Yesterday, Phillipa's Mum had come into the classroom in the morning irate and asking for me. TTA told her I was on a course and she had gone straight down to the headteacher.

Apparently, on Wednesday night, after the headteacher had spoken to Phillipa's Mum about her apparent confession about getting locked in the attic, Phillipa had gone home and said to her Mum that I had asked her if she gets hit at home. She said to her Mum that I'd told Phillipa, if she ever gets hurt or is scared at home that she should tell me and I would call the police who would take her and her sister away for good. I am so glad that I wasn't in yesterday because it sounds like her Mum came in absolutely livid, understandably, and I think she might've punched me! The headteacher had told Phillipa's Mum that I would certainly not have said that and discussed the safeguarding protocols with her. So I met with Phillipa and her Mum first thing this morning in the classroom before everyone else came in and I was really open about what had happened and her Mum was much calmer and understanding. We talked to Phillipa about the severity of what she had said and she said that she had seen it on TV or something. This has really shaken me, what an incredible lie to tell that must have terrified her Mum.

**Saturday 22nd May**

Spent the day with Di today. We had a shop, some lunch and then watched Disney all afternoon. I bloody love my sister. She's moving in with Maximus and I am SO excited for her!

**Sunday 23rd May**

Spent the whole day writing reports. This is insanity.

**Monday 24th May**

Urgh. Claudio had a nosebleed today, which isn't completely uncommon for him. However, I inadvertently pulled a blood clot out that just kept coming and coming and I was nearly sick in his face. It was about the length of my little finger. Like I said, urgh.

(Bed time: 9pm. I'm now officially in bed before the sun sets)

**Tuesday 25th May**

Clarence's Mum came to the door this morning for drop off and I was under instruction from the terrifying office staff to remind her to go to the office to pay for tomorrow's forest school trip to the woods. She's been very evasive, but also has really low levels of literacy so needs all the letters we send out verbally. I've spent so many days at the door helping her understand things that are coming up and payments that are needed and she's generally really open to being helped. Not that it matters but she's from the gypsy roman traveller community and is as blunt as can be so she intimidates me a tad! So she popped along this morning and I said "ooh, the office staff have asked me if you could nip down to see them this morning to pay for tomorrow's trip please?" She said "oh shit I forgot" and promptly pulled a wad of notes out of her bra and brandished them at me! Urgh! I am not touching anything that has come out of your massive chest chasm, thank you very much! I hope this didn't show in my face but I'm relatively expressive so she may have seen my disgust. I politely reminded her that I wasn't able to accept cash and that she'd be better sorting it out with the office so that she could sign the forms at the same time. She shrugged and waddled off down to the office, thank goodness. Close one.

**Wednesday 26th May**

Betty sneezed in my face today. Literally in my face. We stared at each other for a while as I tried to not be sick. I feel another cold coming on. Children are disgusting.

The class trip to the woods, aside from the contagion, was a total success, in most respects! Everyone had so much fun, even Pippin who didn't much fancy being away from technology all day. They sulked for a large portion of the day but ended up playing a marathon game of hide and seek with Rahul, who kept shouting at me "Young, Young! Pip? Pip?" Adorable. There were some issues of poo, which I now consider my daily life, though this time it was animal based. At school, we check the outside area daily before the children come in to make sure it's safe, but I don't suppose you can check an entire wooded area! Katerina was hell-bent on killing every tiny creature. She sat for ages telling me about how she killed an ant and she was so proud of herself. We had a discussion about kindness and how animals feel pain and fear too...well, I discussed, she completely ignored me and kept reiterating how good it was that this ant was now dead. That's a future serial killer right there.

The staff were amazing. They helped the children in groups to build fires and I was so terrified of using tools with them, but because of how seriously the staff took it and sold it to the children they were all golden. Apart from Blake, who didn't get the first turn at helping and his Dad had to carry him off before he set the whole group on fire.

I don't think this class have ever looked so tired by 2pm on a Wednesday! They trudged back to the coach with mud everywhere and flushed cheeks from running around, and most of them fell asleep the instant the coach set off. On the return journey to school, I was sat right at the back in the middle. Musaaleh was sat next to me and after a whole day of me asking him to pull his trousers up, I was considering suggesting to his parents that they get him a belt. I looked over as he had slumped down in his seat, and his trousers were down round his knees! He was looking out of the window, watching the world go by, completely unaware (or unconcerned) that he was effectively sitting on a coach in his pants. I pointed this out to him and he just smiled and shrugged at me! So I suggested he pull his trousers up. He sighed heavily and pulled them up half-heartedly to around his crotch area, then went back to staring out of the window! Maybe he's just not in to trousers. Thank goodness he left his pants on. Thank goodness he was wearing pants in the first place!

**Thursday 27th May**

Oh thank goodness it's the last day of the half term for me (I've got the day off to MOVE HOUSE TOMORROW!!); it's been an interesting one. I've been hugged, kicked, spat out, yelled at, proposed to, invited for dinner (these are all children) and I cannot tell you how tired I am. It's so funny seeing the teachers so happy and the parents so gutted! I was a lucky one, my Mum absolutely loved having us home for holidays and we always did fun things, but I know it's not like that for everyone. The behaviour of a couple of children has deteriorated this week as the holiday has drawn closer and I know it's because they're dreading being at home for the week in an unhappy situation. It makes me so sad that not everyone had the love that I had growing up.

Nevertheless, hello half term, welcome to me. Sadly, I'm going to have to spend the whole week balancing moving house and writing reports, so it won't be a rest at all, but such is life. I always look forward to the holidays because I don't need to hear my name repeated several thousand times a day and often with the vowel sounds elongated.

Miss.... Yooooooouuuuunnnnnngggggwoooooooooooooood argh for goodness sake! It's only three syllables, just say it!

**Friday 28th May**

Being a teacher, we're so lucky to have so much holiday (though much of it should be called overtime), but the downside is we don't get to choose when we have said holidays. So I was not expecting to be able to have today off for moving, I figured I'd go after work to collect the keys and then do it over the weekend. But joy of joys we DO get a moving day! I was SO excited. The main thing that hit me when Mum and I walked in was how much the house stank of smoke. It had always smelled pretty good the few times we'd been, so I guess her use of plug in air fresheners did their job marvellously. We didn't bring anything over today to unpack, instead we spent the whole day cleaning. Not so much fun but I appreciate the time we have because there was no chain. We cleaned things I didn't even consider would need cleaning! I'm imagining next time I move, I'll have to clean whilst all the furniture etc gets moved in because at that moment, someone else will be moving into my old house. I still can't quite believe it's mine, though Mum kept saying 'ours'!

**Saturday 29th May**

Mum has had two of my Grandparents' old sofas in the lounge for ages. They were gifted to her when they got new ones so have been our sofas for a while, but a few months ago, Mum bought some new ones and said we could keep the old sofas for me for my new house. So for months, poor Mum (and me...!) have had four sofas squished into her lounge. Well, today they were finally rehomed! All of the crap I've been storing in Di's old bedroom got moved out so not only do I get a shiny new house (that still smells of cigarettes urgh), Mum also gets something similar!

As this is my first house, there wasn't too much huge furniture to move, so we hired a van ourselves. Dad is down for the weekend to help and Eddie came too, along with my mate Stan who I've known my whole life. I was so grateful for him because his spatial awareness is incredible, so I left him and Eddie to manoeuvre the sofas and the bed through the house and round some pretty narrow spaces. It was a slightly backwards day for gender equality if I'm honest. The men did a lot of the heavy lifting, whilst my Dad unpacked stuff and Mum and Di went round doing things that I didn't think were priorities, but turned out to be crucial for me staying in my new house for the first night, like sorting out curtains and bedding! As a team, though, we absolutely nailed it so I don't suppose it matters who did what.

It was a really busy day and we were pretty knackered at the end. But we popped down to the chippy to get dinner and then I purposefully didn't invite anyone to stay over. I have always been slightly nervous of the dark after watching The Exorcist when I was about 12 and in my first year of university, I woke up in the middle of one night to find a man halfway through my window. I've never been able to sleep on the ground floor since and still get a bit twitchy if I hear the curtains blowing against an open window at night. Because of all this, I was determined to stay in my own house alone to ensure that I wasn't scared and wouldn't **need** someone else to be with me.

**<u>Sunday 30th May</u>**

You know that feeling where you wake up and you can't figure out where you are? That was me last night. About 6 times! Went down this morning and realised I'd left the back door unlocked all night, great start. How am I ever going to be a proper grownup in my own home?! My own home. I can't believe this is my house. I obviously couldn't have bought it without my parents' help; they've been so generous and helpful and have always encouraged me to work hard and save. Plus, Mum has been letting me live in her house rent free since I got back from uni with the understanding that I save that money for the house instead. So here I am, a home owner and already screwing up and inviting criminals into my house! Must. Lock. Doors.

Noted.

**Tuesday 1st June**

Have spent the last couple of days decorating. Mum had suggested I do this before moving in so that we didn't need to move furniture around but I was too eager to get in. She was, of course, annoyingly correct. But never mind! I'm starting with my bedroom and it's really helped to get some extra cigarette smell out of it. I've also bought some stickers to go on some walls; I've done a purple feature wall behind the bed and then put some stickers of musical notes running along the wall. It looks awesome and I'm really pleased with it! Because they worked out so well I've bought some red flower stickers to go in the lounge – it's all textured paint down there and will be a nightmare to take off or paint, so this is an easy win.

My only gripe is that somehow whilst decorating I hit my ear on a paint can on the floor, which Di finds hilarious and won't stop bringing up. Humph.

**Wednesday 2nd June**

Did some work in the garden today. I've had to confront my hatred of lawn mowers because hey, no one else is going to do it now! I suddenly felt another huge surge of appreciation for Mum doing all this stuff with me not helping one bit. Gran, Grandad and my Uncle came over today too. Gran bought me some heathers to plant in the garden and we all had a bit of a go at hauling out the torrent of weeds that had taken over. There is so much more garden than we realised! It's not big by any means, but there's a patch of lawn, a flower bed and a little patio at the end, so it's pretty perfect for me. There's also the asbestos shed, but I'm mostly ignoring that until a point where we decide to get it taken down.

**Thursday 3rd June**

Report writing, which sucks, but did it in my very own house, which rocks!

**Friday 4th June**

FINISHED MY REPORTS TODAY!!!! We're told to proof read our own before sending them to our designated proof reader in school, but it's so difficult to see anything other than what your brain knows you were trying to write! I've had a look through all of them but it's cursory and I'm sure there are many mistakes yet to be found. I am exhausted. I've calculated that it takes about two hours to write each report, then time for proof reading and editing, then time for printing and enveloping. All in all, I think each report takes about three hours, which is ninety hours per class, which is ninety hours on top of the 40-60 hour weeks we already work. I reckon parents will skim through them in about thirty seconds.

**Saturday 5th June**

Went shopping with Mum and Di today for loads of other things I need for the house, ahem, **my** house. We went to some charity shops to find things like a TV stand and dining room chairs etc. and got a really good haul from the British Heart Foundation! Then to Argos, trusty old Argos, for bookcases and a dining room table. I did of course also buy many more ridiculous pretty things that are not necessary but I'm really excited about; candles and vases etc. I'm going to have to go slow with lots of things, like a spare bed, because I don't have the money to fully furnish an entire house all in one week and it is infuriating; I am not patient.

**Sunday 6th June**

It's been so busy this week in a really great way, but I forgot to relax and enjoy myself and now I have that Sunday night feeling ahead of going back to work tomorrow! I tried baking today in my new oven (just to clarify, the oven is old, but it is new to me) and it is very different from Mum's, so everything was simultaneously burnt and raw. I won't be taking these things to work tomorrow to show that I am a domestic Goddess in her new abode.

# Chapter 6
# Summer term 2

**Monday 7th June**
Yikes, we got told in today's staff meeting that I'm going to be moving to Year 2 next year. I'm not sure how I feel about it. Scratch that, I know exactly how I feel about it. It's scary, the children are older, the work is harder (yes I know they're still only 6 and 7 years old but still!) and it's a completely different curriculum.

I'm amazed at how many parents saw this and congratulated me on getting a promotion. Contrary to popular belief, me now teaching Year 2 instead of Reception does not mean a promotion! The Year Six teachers are not necessarily the best paid in the school, this is not how salary works.

The other thing we talked about in the staff meeting is the fact that this week the Year 1s will start going through the Phonics Screening Check. I had a chat with the Phonics Lead this morning to see if I could sit in on a couple as I haven't seen them before, but this is what they're working towards throughout Reception and Year 1 so I should probably know more.

**Tuesday 8th June**
I introduced my little lovelies to 3d shapes today. I regret it. Gary came running up to me waving a cube around like a maniac and said "Look Miss Youngwood it's a pube!" No matter how many times I correct him, he has gone home telling his grandmother than he learned all about pubes today.

I may well be arrested.

**Wednesday 9th June**
I spent a bit of time in Year 2 today after Monday's news that I would be teaching up there next year. It helped a bit to alleviate

some of my anxiety about it. Reception is full of lunatics, where there are children all over the place all the time. It's loud and messy and I love it, but it was actually a lovely change of pace to go into key stage 1 where they are all together. They all sit on the carpet together, when they go to activities, they all go to their own tables and it feels a lot calmer. I'm going to have to re-educate myself on a lot of things; they were doing the Great Fire of London today and whilst I could identify the basics, I'm definitely going to need a facts refresher before I teach it next year! Overall, I think it's going to be a lot of fun; they're a lot more independent, they understood my humour a bit more and it was easier to read most of their work!

**Thursday 10th June**

So. Phonics Screening Checks. It all sounds a bit strange to me. Putting six-year-olds in a room with an adult and being asked to sound out and read new words...that part I get, I'm not an idiot, it's a good summative assessment of the Phonics they have learned in the year and whether or not they can apply the skills. If they pass it, great, if not they have to repeat it at the end of Year 2. But as far as I can understand it and from what I've seen from observing a few, during the actual process you're not allowed to smile at them indicatively or tell them if they've read the word correctly or not. They're not allowed to use anything to help them and the adults are almost transformed into robots so as to not lead them in their answers. This sounds a bit cold for a six-year old.

Also, there's no assessment whatsoever for assessing their spelling to go with this, and children have been having interventions for weeks to 'practise' for the Phonics screen... is this the best use of their time? Do we need them to read a list of 40 words or do we want them to read words in context and experience joy from reading such words, by escaping into a story or learning a fact? The children who were confident with their phonics sped through them and looked like they quite enjoyed it because they knew it was something they are good at. The couple I saw who weren't so confident, however, looked stressed and the teacher stopped one assessment a few words in because they barely got any right – at least this seems kinder. I'm not sure about this at all.

It also gave me more of a chance to look through the Year 1 programme for Phonics – Phase 5 – and holy moly there is so much to teach in that year! No wonder there's so much pressure on Reception to learn Phases 2-4. The pace is incredible and whilst I've been able to spend other lessons going back over concepts they've needed more time on, there's no such allowance in Phonics. You have a few minutes at the start of each twenty minute session to recap all the sounds they've already learned and then you move on, learning 3, 4 or 5 new sounds a week! Lots of the children are coping and are mostly picking it all up and I like to think that my training at university and on placements has helped me develop quality teaching strategies, but there are some that are struggling to keep up and whilst I've popped them into regular interventions, I worry about them.

**Friday 11th June**

Quote of the day – "Miss, it's SO hot today. It's so hot that it's like the inside of a chip, that's how hot it is!" Couldn't have put it better myself, Claudio.

(Bed time: 9pm but impossible to sleep in this heat)

**Sunday 13th June**

I hate camping. I love nature, I love the countryside, but I hate camping. Why would anyone choose to sleep on the floor? I could do it when I was 17, but now I'm that tiny bit older my hips hurt and my back hurts and I just don't want to sleep on the floor! I don't get drunk enough to just pass out like Eddie does. However, when your boyfriend's mate can get you free VIP tickets to Download, you camp.

I've never done a weekend festival before. I've been to Slam Dunk and the Vans Warped Tour, but just for a day each time. I was really excited to go to Download and there were loads of bands I wanted to see, so I was really grateful and chuffed to have been invited. Eddie, on the other hand, is a festival veteran. He's been able to show me the ropes and give me good tips on how to survive! We had such a great time eating and drinking and listening to music and hanging out with his mates. Download is pretty notorious for the weather though; it's either boiling or torrential rain and this year we got boiling. I gotta say, I'm not desperate to rush back to sleeping in a tent when it's 30 degrees and your tent-mate is consistently exuding beer fumes.

**Monday 14th June**

I'm so tired from the weekend and sometimes tiredness can have strange effects on your brain, so I thought I'd gone mad when getting the children to write simple, descriptive sentences using different adjectives today, I came across this:

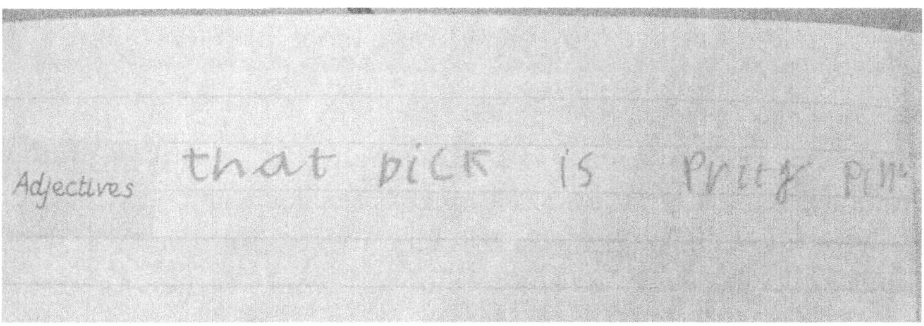


Apart from the missing full stop (livid, we've been working on those for months), I was half amused and half ready to call social services. I asked Francisco to read the sentence to me or tell me what they meant, but they could do neither. So I have no idea what the intended sentence here was. I just ticked it and sent it home.

**Tuesday 15th June**

When it gets hot, most adults will want to lie down and be very quiet for a long time. Children do not want this. For themselves or for anyone else! They struggle with the concept of stillness on a regular day, but when they're hot it's like every fibre of their being needs to move more. Here are the problems with hot days I've noticed so far with the temperature rising:

- There will be a lovely redheaded vampire in your class who never comes with a hat or sun cream and you watch them like a hawk expecting them to burst into flames at any given moment.
- There will be at least one, if not two, who bring their sun cream to school and try to take a bath in it every six minutes.
- It takes twenty minutes to start the next lesson after a break because everyone is queued at the water fountain trying to fill their bottles up.
- They still want to hug you. If anyone tells you children don't sweat, it's a lie.
- If your classroom has the sun in the afternoon, it's like having a party in a greenhouse.
- At least three children will regularly go and stick their head under the cold tap. I can't blame them for this.

**Wednesday 16th June**

There's been so more teacher bashing on social media this week. People are pissed that we get 13 weeks holiday a year. This is true. However, we are paid for 32.5 hours a week and generally work somewhere between 40 and 60 hours a week. If you work in an office and work double your hours, do you get paid extra or get time back in lieu? Well, we get time back in the form of the children's holidays. However, I haven't had one holiday yet where I have done no work. I've had to use the time to catch up on updating the children's learning journeys, planning, entering data or in school setting up the classroom. I spent most of the May half term writing reports. So yes we get 13 weeks holiday a year, but no teacher will have 13 weeks unearned or in its entirety. I'm assuming it comes from jealously or insecurity but it's infuriating that people judge what they don't know. I'd love to see these people teach 30 children every day and not need regular breaks! Especially when it's as hot as the sun in your classroom.

**Thursday 17th June**

TTA and I started the year really strict with the children about tidying up. We did the whole routine of 'this is your classroom and you need look after it". We taught them to respect themselves, each other and our property (though Blake cannot manage this; he's still going into crisis on a daily basis) and have reinforced this throughout the year. They've been pretty great as a whole, of course there's always a couple that have zero interest in being helpful but as soon as there are rewards involved good lord can they pick up Lego! Jonah is always keen to help, however he has Autism and sometimes I forget that he takes things rather literally. Today, when we were tidying up, I was giving out directions as to where some children could focus their attention. You know the ones; "Claudio check out the book corner", "Phillipa, get down on the floor" etc. When I instructed Jonah to "get under the table" he did. I turned back round a minute or so later and bless him, there he was, sat obediently under the table, probably wondering why on earth I was making him sit under a table! Ah I love this kid.

**Friday 18th June**

Jim put a chair leg on top of my foot today whilst sitting on it. It was an accident but when I cried out in pain he just moved the chair, then went back to his Lego! The conversation went like this:

"Jim, I'm ok but did you know your chair was on my foot?"

He nodded, totally unconcerned.

"Even when it's an accident, do you know what you should say if you hurt someone?"

"Yes."

"...Ok so you need to say you're sorry."

"Ok. Sorry."

It could not have been less empathetic, but better than nowt I suppose.

Come hither, weekend.

**Saturday 19th June**

Went out for a mate's birthday last night. I can't remember how much wine we drank but I never want to drink ever again.

At some point this morning, Eddie shouted to me from the lounge window that there were a few ducks waddling along the path, so I went and opened the front door to have a look. Sure enough, there were four ducks just wandering along. They saw the door was open, or that I was there, and turned down the path and started walking up to the house!! I had to shut the door before they came in. I grew up listening to Beatrix Potter so there's a small part of me that thinks I could've invited them in for tea and a civilised conversation.

**Sunday 20th June**

Dad's been down here for a few days so we got to do Father's Day locally today. Di and I decided that a really great idea would be a Sunday roast on a canal boat in Birmingham. SUCH a great idea...when it's not the hottest day of the year. 35degrees. Who on earth wants to sit in a greenhouse and eat boiling hot food on the hottest day of the year?! It was a lovely couple of hours relaxing on a canal boat and a really great thing to do, but just the wrong day to do it. Man did we sweat. We got him a big badge that said World's Best Dad though and he wore it proudly all day, so I think that made up for it...

**Monday 21st June**

Oh good. Another 13 hour day. Thank you for that. We invited next year's Nursery and Reception parents in for a meeting to talk to them about what we do and everything that will happen, but of course it didn't start until 6pm and I didn't leave until gone 7.30. So. Tired. They were a lovely bunch to be fair, with lots of questions! Lots of them concerned about handwriting and spelling and the pace of their child moving through the reading scheme. What is it with parents and reading? Does nobody read for pleasure anymore? We had about two-thirds of the parents show up so we know that most people got the messages. When we looked at the list of people who couldn't come, only a couple had called to say they couldn't make it because of childcare or work, and the rest of the parents were apparently not a surprise to the headteacher based on their previous engagement!

We're bringing in home visits next year, so that's exciting. It'll be really interesting to see where each child comes from and will hopefully develop that family-school bond more quickly, though I can imagine some parents are going to really worry about having us come into their home. I say us, it won't be me as I'll be in Year 2! I'm a bit gutted, I'd love to go snooping round everyone's houses.

**Tuesday 22nd June**

I was having a lovely chat with Betty today when she suddenly ran off towards her best friend. I turned round, and they were in the role play wearing all seventeen hats at once but no trousers. I don't really know what to make of this or what else even happened today.

(Bed time: 8.45pm. My friends are mocking me for going to bed in broad daylight)

**Wednesday 23rd June**

BADRA CAN READ! Remember Badra? The g / ssssss / g / ssssss debacle? She can now read! I'm a genius, this is my biggest accomplishment this year, though I'm not even sure I can claim it as my own accomplishment because she's the one who has learned to read but I am SO proud of her! She's nailed three letter words, can read a lot of four letter words and even has some tricky words under her belt. YES BADRA! Now if only Rahul could say my full name we'll be in business!

**Thursday 24th June**

I suggested to some of the staff that we pop to the pub after work tomorrow. A few people seemed interested, a few already had plans, and one said "Oh no I can't, I always meet my husband after work on a Friday and we do the food shop." When I suggested she perhaps do it another time this week she smiled as though I'd just offended her and said sorry, then turned and walked away! If I ever get that rigid about when I do the food shop I'll request to be slapped.

I never know whether to invite the headteacher or not to things like this. We get on well, but is it appropriate for them to come to the pub with the staff? She tends to stay out of the staffroom at lunchtime, I'm not sure if that's because it's inappropriate or whether she just doesn't have time. It's a weird one. Based on people's responses I don't think we'll end up going tomorrow anyway. I'm quite proud of myself for asking people to do something sociable. I automatically default to thinking that people don't like me and tend to avoid social situations so that they're not given the chance to hate me to my face. It was really huge to ask people to do something with me outside of work. Though, I'm not sure any of us have got much in common other than work and I don't really want to go out after work and just talk about work! Either way, I took a big step and I will try to not take it to heart if it doesn't happen.

**Friday 25th June**

Another non-uniform day. I don't think the people who organise these days realise how mental the children go when they're in their own clothes! The premise for today is that they could wear their own clothes if they brought in a summer fair donations. I'm not sure everyone read the brief. I stayed until about 7pm tonight putting raffle tickets on prizes so nobody could be bothered to go to the pub after that. There were a couple of things I wanted to just take home immediately, so I might have to buy some raffle tickets next week! So very tired, I've clocked in at about 60 hours this week. Time for bed.

**Saturday 26th June**
When I envisaged meeting Eddie's parents, I pictured us having dinner together or meeting in the pub for a drink. A nice chat for an hour or two, tick, then head home and do it again in another month or so. I did not quite bank on an entire weekend staying with them in their holiday cottage! They have a place down in Devon that they use for weekends and holidays and then rent out if they're not using it, so Eddie had suggested he and I take a trip down there. We'd gone through our diaries and found we were both free this weekend, but when he checked it with them they said they were already planning on going down then, but we should go too and we could all meet...how do you say no to that?!

I was so nervous but they are absolutely lovely, hurray! It was a bit awkward meeting them, Eddie had warned me that being a cockney and a Scot they aren't particularly physical, but in the absence of a handshake or a hug you just kind of smile at each other and say hi and I find it really uncomfortable! But introductions were made, then his mum suggested we go to the ferry boat, to which I got very excited as I love boats...she laughed...hard. She was talking about the pub.

**Sunday 27th June**
We spent much of yesterday in the pub and wandering around Shaldon, a pleasant seaside village. Today, we went on the actual ferry boat across to Teignmouth and found another pub. I really like how Eddie's parents do their weekends! We had a wander round and along the pier and then Eddie and I set off back for home. It's been quite intense and I was so nervous the whole time, but they're both so lovely. Eddie's mum often comes out with little facts or hilarious stories, and his dad will then question where she got her facts, they're so funny together.

**Monday 28th June**
Don't judge me, but Blake is on a respite retreat this week and I feel so calm and relaxed. Don't get me wrong, I want the best for him, but it has taken so much pressure off just knowing that he won't be in and I don't have to worry. I don't sleep particularly well

nowadays with the anxiety and never sleep particularly well on a Sunday night, but last night was a lot better than usual with the knowledge that he wouldn't be in. You could kind of feel the children relax too, when we did the register and I said he wouldn't be in for a couple of days. Imran actually closed her eyes and sighed in relief! I hate how the children have been so affected by all of the incidents we've had with him. I still don't know how to handle it all so trying to help other, younger people try to cope is so tricky!

Today has been lovely. It was One World Day, where we were celebrating where everyone is from, their cultures, traditions and beliefs. The school had a few parents come in and go to each class to talk about any particular celebrations or food or traditions they have. It was so interesting! We had a Mum come in to tell us about China. She showed us how to eat with chopsticks and had brought us all fortune cookies. We had a grandmother tell us about wearing saris and showed the children how to put one on by using me as a model – my first time in a sari and it was so beautiful and comfy! We had another mum talk to us about Poland (I want to go immediately) and we had someone's uncle tell us all about Pakistan (I learned so much). It was so interesting and wonderful to hear more about where our children are from. Dasha told us a lot about Turkey and where some of her family still live and what they get up to when they go to visit. Bernard told us, in his broken English, about the Jamaican food they eat and for someone who normally just smiles and laughs or nods along, it was amazing to hear him talk about his family meal times. We really need to make more of this, our families have such diverse backgrounds and other than an initial questionnaire when they enter the school we don't do enough to celebrate them or get to know them.

**Tuesday 29th June**

Oh my goodness. We did a little reflective lesson today, on people who are special to us. We read a story and we talked about their parents or other family members, someone suggested the lollipop lady for helping to keep them safe crossing the road, which was adorable. When we came to record our ideas about who is special to them and why, Frances, who has been a royal pain in the butt this year, wrote this:

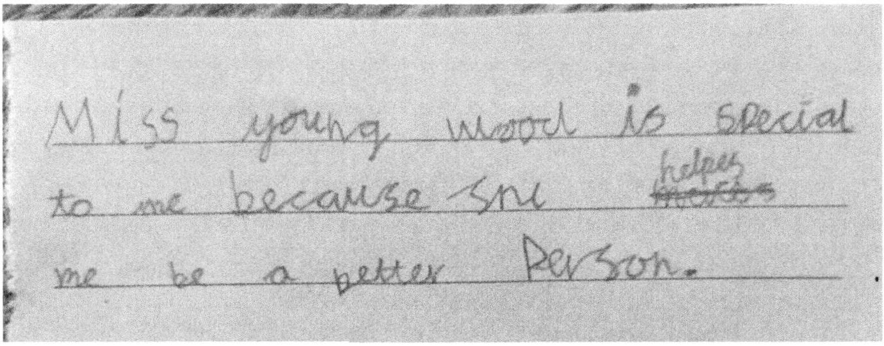

Miss young wood is special to me because she helps me be a better Person.

I nearly wept all over that child. How gorgeous is that! I'm actually making a difference in children's lives. Well, one at least.

**Wednesday 30th June**

I've done so little today. I'm tired and it's absolutely boiling and I just could not be bothered. It'll bite me in the butt later on in the week but it's nearly the end of the year so who cares right...!

(Bed time: 9pm. It's genuinely tricky to sleep in so much daylight. Nobody understands my troubles.)

**Thursday 1st July**

Some people might find it strange that I often called children by their title and surname. You are a superstar, Miss Ramsbottom, well done. Excuse me, Mr Plank, could you tuck your chair in please? Miss Fickle, tuck your shirt in please. I've found it helps the younger children to identify and remember their last name (yes some children had no idea what their last name was in September), helps them to understand what relation 'Miss' and 'Youngwood' have to my name, and also brings a sense of decorum to the practice.

Mr Patek, the happiest five-year-old with the biggest smile you would ever meet, LOVES this. He giggles infectiously every time I used his full name and sometimes even requested I say it if I'd accidentally just used his first name instead. "Darpan, could you pass me that pen please?" "Um, don't you mean Mr Patek?" ... "Sorry, you're absolutely right. Mr Patek, please pass me that pen!" He loves it so much, that a month or so ago, I turned a piece of work over to see who it belonged to and yes, there on the back, were the words Mr Patek. He started referring to himself in the third person as Mr Patek and writing it on his work, though we had to have a conversation today because it was further changed to Mr P! This child is glorious and it makes me smile to think about him introducing himself to people as Mr Patek or Mr P.

**Friday 2nd July**

My very first school summer fair as a teacher! It was great fun, though very much like the Christmas fair, except with no Santa Claus. We told the parents they could come and collect their children from 2pm and then we had all the stalls ready to go until 6pm. There were food trucks and a bouncy castle, face painting and glittery tattoos, games and a DJ! It was such a summer party out in the playground, I had a great time! I took the children who hadn't been picked up early round some of the stalls with their purses and wallets, then the after-school club collected them at 3.30 and I went off to my stall.

I took over on the bottle tombola at exactly the right time. A parent who has a child in Nursery came with his eye on the bottle of tequila that was front and centre. At first, he let his daughter pick the tickets. £1 for three, not too shabby. She won a bottle of squash. They had another go and she got nothing, so they went off. Literally 30 seconds went by and the Dad came back by himself (I guess the daughter had gone off with her Mum...I hope!). He bought three rounds of tickets, then gave me a fiver. He won a couple of bottles of wine and a couple of bottles of soft drinks. He conceded defeat, I got him a plastic bag and off he went. Then, no more than five minutes later he was back and handed over a tenner! He kept playing and playing and playing and 'won' almost every bottle there but not the tequila! His wife came over and pointed out that for the amount he'd spent, he could've just gone to the shops and bought a bottle of the same tequila. They stayed a while longer and in the end, he'd spent £40 just at the bottle tombola, so we just gave him the tequila! That's a lovely chunk of money going into the school pot, well done that man!

I am so impressed with the generosity of our parents and how wonderful our staff are. Whether you're a teacher or not, odds are you're going to be pretty tired by 5pm on a Friday, but everyone was smiling and joking and full of energy until the very end. The parents and children seemed to have a great time and we raised so much money for the school. What a day.

**Saturday 3rd July**

I'm so tired. I know I moan about it a lot and I don't want to be that person that's always complaining that they're tired, but now I have my own house I don't need to tell anyone else that I'm so tired! I can just stay in and watch tv and nobody will judge me. Bliss. I've been steadily meeting my neighbours in the last few weeks and they all seem so lovely. The houses across the road are all tiny bungalows inhabited by old ladies, and they're really sweet too. Also handy to have some built in neighbourhood watch! There's a family of four to one side of me; I met the wife last week and she suggested we all have dinner sometime. God I hope she was just being polite. They seem nice enough but I'm not sure my social anxiety can cope with that! Then there's a gorgeous old couple to the other side of me, who have been graciously accepting my many, many, many parcels since I moved in without complaint!

I'd planned to do a whole lot of nothing today, but needed a basic shop top up so I nipped over the shops. When I got home, I walked up the path to find Mum in the flowerbed. She just cannot get enough of gardening and I love her for it, but it kind of put an end to my lazy day!

**Sunday 4th July**

Eddie is in a heavy metal band and they played last night so I went to see them. It was so amazing to see him play bass and he's absolutely incredible, but I'll be honest, I hate the music! I really like rock and metal, but this is too heavy for me. They seemed to really enjoy themselves though and it was awesome to see; Eddie often plays guitar when he's hanging out and he's so talented, not that he believes that.

One of his mates has a new girlfriend and I met her last night and I absolutely adore her! She was instantly warm and fun and interesting, and because I'd had a drink I asked her to her face what she was doing dating Leon because he can be a bit of a bellend! She just laughed and I think now we're friends and that I'm in love with her.

**Monday 5th July**

I overheard a Dad of a Year 2 child in the playground after school. She was telling him all about how they've been practising for sports day tomorrow and she's so excited about it. To my horror, he said "well I can't be there but remember if you win, I'll buy you an iPhone." He wasn't kidding. What the hell?! First of all, I don't even have an iPhone, never mind this 7-year-old. Second of all, maybe try to encourage her to enjoy it and not to be a sore loser? Douche.

**Tuesday 6th July**

Sports day. Groan.

How everyone feels about sports day is pretty much a 50/50 split with the people who take part (teachers, parents and children). It doesn't matter what age you are; some people are sporty, well-coordinated and love a physical challenge (you want me to climb that tree to rescue the flyaway plastic bag? No problem! Shall I just bend down to get that piece of paper off the floor without bending my knees? Easy!) and some people aren't. Some people can fall over while they're sitting down. Remember the Wii Fit? In case you're wondering, surprise surprise, I'm in the latter category. I can sprint, I'm pretty speedy, but (as previously mentioned eighteen times) I'm super clumsy and not well coordinated. That's a problem when you're having to do a few things at once, like the egg and spoon race or something else similar to coordinate your ability to carry something as well as run. I also forgot that I'm getting older and I can't just sprint without warming up and stretching first, but since there's no way to do this before the teacher's race without being the tool who's taking it really seriously, I just jumped into it and pulled a few thousand muscles.

*It's the taking part that counts!* It's not though, is it? It's about winning. That's why you award stickers or points or medals. To the **winners**. Some schools might give a 'good effort' or an 'I tried' sticker to the others but there are too many losers to do this with consistently. It's not about taking part. You take part to win. This is an important lesson to teach children though (the taking part bit, not the winning), as one of many lies you tell children until they're old enough to realise the truth. Boy oh boy can some people not handle losing though! I was not prepared for all tantrums, storm offs, refusals and altogether mayhem that is sports day – and that's just the teachers trying to get out of doing a teacher race! You can put the children in mixed ability teams, but somehow there always ends up being a team that win every round and a team that lose every round. I clapped and cheered, the parents clapped and cheered, but deep down those non-sporty children know that they're just a step away from falling over and I had to find a way to help those children through the emotional torment and savagery that is sports day. Unless you're a sporty type, in which case, you'd probably love the whole day. Full disclosure, I hate these people. They are the worst.

We have also spent a number of weeks practising the events. I'm not sure there was any reason for individuals to have no idea which bean bag to collect in what order after so many practise runs. Perhaps the crowds threw them off or just the knowledge that whatever they did, they wouldn't be able to beat the red team.

I guess there might be some really lucky teachers who work in a school where sports day can take place in the sight of some familiar toilets (oh the dreams I have as a teacher!). However, my school does not. So we got all of the children into some high visibility jackets, tried to avoid it as adults but resigned ourselves to setting a good example and begrudgingly put them on, and trudged 120 pupils over to our closest primary school that had the luxury of their own field. I was not prepared for the many, many bathroom runs that ensued! Often just as a race is about to start. We had planned in a rest stop in between some of the activities so that we could all go at once, but you can't always get children to time their bladders. My terrifying TA would often say "just try, have a squeeze," and I loved this saying! These are my two main memories from my first sports day as a teacher; tantrums and toilets.

The highlight of the day? The toddler race. We might as well have held a drunk and disoriented race (but probably couldn't actually have done this, I don't think parents need encouragement to bring a bucks fizz picnic or a bottle of white lightning to their child's sports day). They swayed and they waddled and some hilariously turned round and ran back to the start! Some even made a break for freedom and I really enjoyed sitting with my athletes (and wailing non-athletes) watching the parents chase after their tearaways across the field! Good times.

(Bed time: fell asleep on the sofa at 7pm)

**<u>Wednesday 7th July</u>**

Wow my legs are tight from yesterday's staff race. Thank goodness for PPA so I could basically just sit down all day. I went up to the classroom at the end of the day but had to just sit down again and asked the children to do jobs for me. They're very keen and now I can see why people might have their own children. There are often times at home when I turn to ask someone to bring me the remote and realise that I'm home alone and that won't fly. Eddie is pretty great at passing me things when we're together but he really mocks me for it. I'm not sure how he's got a leg to stand on, he showed me a makeshift grabber he'd made so that he could reach things in his house without getting out of bed!

**<u>Thursday 8th July</u>**

We had to send Blake home today. He came in absolutely fine, chatting about what he was going to do over the weekend, excited that he was going to go on a real train. Then at about 10.30, just before we stopped for snack, I went over to quietly warn him that we would soon be stopping for snack and did he want to be in charge of ringing the tambourine to get everyone's attention. He went into full crisis in less than a second. The computer is smashed, he broke the interactive whiteboard, there were books everywhere, drinks bottles thrown at children, chairs overturned, tables pushed over, you name it he threw or punched or broke it. We had to evacuate all the other children and I ended up having to restrain him. It was the most awful feeling and I'm not sure who's heart was beating faster, mine or his. I eventually got him to calm down and the deputy came to help me, but as soon as he left with his Mum I burst into tears. The anxiety and fear and the feeling of having utterly failed a child is so present every single day that I just don't know how to cope with this. The management decision was for him to come back in on Monday so, as awful as it sounds, I can relax a bit tomorrow.

**<u>Friday 9th July</u>**

There is a group of children who are absolutely nailing Phonics, some that are doing just fine, and some that have no idea what sounds are in their name. We were writing instructions today for how to get ready in the morning and this little gem came to light:
"Pull your tits up." How very dare you, kid! You pull yours up! I'll have you know I am only twenty-two and have no need for such an

instruction! I obviously took it very personally. However, she had mistakenly used the 'i' as the long 'igh' sound to try to spell 'tights' so I forgave her and I am still laughing about this now.

**Saturday 10th July**

I've booked a holiday with a mate to go to Dublin in August for a couple of days, I'm so excited! I love a good holiday and she's so much fun so I'm really looking forward to it. She's one of these people who just exudes fun and joy; we met in school when we were about 14 and I instantly felt a mix of love and jealously for her! That's never really gone away; there isn't a mean or selfish bone in her body and I quite often feel inferior to her. Almost like the imposter syndrome you feel at work, but socially, like why on earth does this person want to spend time with me because I'm so dull and rubbish in comparison! It's a feeling I've had most of my life and it's tricky to navigate, but I'm just focussing on how much fun we'll have.

It's so nice after working so hard to start looking forward to all the nice things I'm going to do in the summer. I'm determined to make the most of it and not just sit around for 6 weeks.

I'm definitely mostly just going to sit around for 6 weeks.

**Sunday 11th July**

I'd ordered a wardrobe for the spare room and it was delivered late yesterday. The final moments of an 8am-8pm delivery slot, ridiculous. It's taken me about 16 hours but I built it all by myself and I am so proud! It's ever so slightly wonky in places but it's awesome and I did it and now my hands hurt. Can I count this as a sporting injury?

**Monday 12th July**

Disappointment number three for the snails came about today, in the form of impending births. As snails are hermaphrodites, there will definitely be a time where they will mate with each other and suddenly I'd end up with not just thirty children, but also forty to sixty baby snails! Unacceptable. I am not Mother Theresa. I barely want the three snails we have at this point, they're an absolute hassle. Their slime got all over the tank and as much as I've tried to get the children to clean it out, they're not having it. So, it's competition time – who wants to adopt a giant African land snail?! You're welcome, parents.

Moral of the story – just don't bother getting a pet. Take a trip to the farm once a year. Job done.

**Tuesday 13th July**

After three months of writing, re-writing, proof reading and re-proof reading, editing and trying desperately to try to reword the phrase "Frasier is a dick sometimes", the reports went home today. The relief was immense but the parents are known to stand in the playground, immediately rip them open and read them. It only took thirty seconds of Johnathan's Mum reading their report to come back to the door and tell me "you've given me someone else's report..." I nearly cried on the spot, I thought I had been so careful and had triple checked them but my worst fear had been realised. How many others were wrong? Who had Johnathan's report and who's was this? Then she said "you've put that they're really polite and helpful. That can't be my child!" I nearly punched her in the face for scaring me. I need wine.

(Bed time: 10pm. I can push it a bit now it's coming to the end of the year! Just a bit though, I'm no owl.)

**Wednesday 14th July**

This is the last time I will have an entire day out of class for admin, as next year it will only be 10% as I won't get ECT time anymore. I'm really sad about it, I get so much done and I know that despite how many weeks I work 50-60 hours instead of my contracted 32.5, next year that will have to increase because of this lost non-contact time. I'm also sad because the government are changing the programme and from next year, new teachers will have two years of this not one!

I celebrated having had such a great year of Wednesdays out of class by collating the names of all the parents who had expressed interest in adopting one of our snails, and at the end of the day we drew them out of a hat to see who would be the lucky ones taking some slime in a shell home. Congratulations Jim, Darpan and Badra! I think I audibly cackled when they were announced.

**Thursday 15th July**

Mehmet's Dad came over to me this morning and asked if we could meet after school to discuss his report. I wasn't entirely surprised, I had been as diplomatic as possible but there's only so many positive ways you can put a spin on a kid who is rude, selfish and has no interest in being a good person. It wasn't this that his Dad wanted to talk about, though. He came into the classroom after all the children had gone home and I had arranged my face into a professional look, and said that he was shocked and disappointed at how I hadn't written Mehmet's report from scratch, instead having just copied and pasted everything from a generic bank of statements. I was really taken aback. Apparently his wife is a school teacher and immediately recognised all of the comments so sent him in to attack me. I hadn't used a comments bank at all, the little pricks, other than for the ability to differentiate between 'is starting to', 'can' and 'confidently'. I calmly explained that I was surprised at his wife's reaction, seeing as I hadn't used a comments bank, to which he interrupted and said 'yes you have'. I can now see why Mehmet has the level of manners he does. I suggested that perhaps his wife recognised many of the statements because they were lifted straight out of the curriculum, as much of it was about Mehmet's competencies within the development matters bands. Everything I said, he just kept rudely insisting that I'd used generic comments banks and had put no thought or effort into it.

I wholly resented this coming from this particular parent, because Mehmet's report had taken almost double the amount of time as some of the others due to me trying to figure out diplomatic, positive phrases to use. I had written personalised strengths and areas for development for every single child and was really upset that I was being accused of something I didn't do, by proxy! He couldn't even have a well-reasoned argument with me because he was there on behalf of his wife! I suggested that she and I have a discussion and he said "oh what's the point" so then I asked him what he needed from our conversation. He repeated that he was shocked and disappointed at the lack of effort on my part and that it showed nothing of what I knew of his son. So there we had it. They had clearly read between the lines of my diplomacy and were pissed that I didn't see him as some do-no-wrong angel, as they did. In the end, I told him that I was really upset by his accusations as each report took hours of my time, but that if he and his wife were truly unhappy with it they were welcome to speak to a member of senior management. I pointed out this might be helpful as they had proofread all of my reports so would be able to competently discuss how similar each one was. He got up in a huff and again, said "what's the point" and stormed out!

What. A. Bellend.

**Friday 16th July**

Ah the snails were rehomed today. That was a quick turnaround and I'm pretty sure the glee on my face was evident when handing them over at the end of the day. Good luck, parents!

**Saturday 17th July**

I'm not sure I can remember a weekend where I felt as relaxed as this. There's very little work to be done in school that is time pressured at the moment, so I managed to sit out in my garden and have a little sunbathe and just enjoy life today! This is a very strange feeling.

Di, Maximus and Eddie came over in the evening and we drank and ate and played Pandemic and we had such a good time. We're planning to go away for the weekend in the summer; we've found a renovated cowshed in Ludlow so we're going to hold up in there for a weekend in August. We've planned the menu and so far, we've got:

Crisps and dips

Brownies (Maximus will make these, hurray!)
Fry up breakfast
Nachos
Pizza, garlic bread and chips
Beige buffet
All the drinks we can think of

This is how I want to spend all future weekends.

**Sunday 18th July**

I am SO EXCITED! We've booked a holiday! And by we, I mean my grandparents. They're so wonderfully generous, they're taking Di, Mum and me away with them and my uncle for a week in Lake Como, Italy. It's my Grandad's birthday on 29th August so we're going for the week around then so we'll be away for his birthday. We've done a few holidays together in the last few years and I always absolutely love them. Recently, they've started booking with a company rather than doing it ourselves, so we're herded on to coaches and told when to be where, which is actually quite nice other than the fact that the company is generally for older people so Di and I spend the week with a coach full of old people. We always have a great time together though, and I plan to eat nothing but pizza, pasta and gelato for the entire week! Hmm...should probably start dieting now to make room for it all.

**Monday 19th July**

Oh my goodness what an emotional day it has been. It's the last week of school. The last week of this class being in the Early Years Foundation Stage. The last week of my first year as a teacher. My last week with the best first class I could ever have imagined teaching. To top it all off, we did a circle time about what the children have liked about this year and what they remember most. Lots of them talked about their friends, which is gorgeous, or the school dinners! When we moved to writing their thoughts down, one little girl wrote this:

"I lik dis yer beecu because I lic mis yunw." (I like this year because I like Miss Youngwood)

Ok, the spelling is atrocious, but the message is so utterly heart-warming. Tears, tears and more tears.

**Tuesday 20th July**

Now, I'm not going to lie, I have no intention of doing any more 'work' with them this week. It is all about transitions, managing change, preparing them for Year 1 and also sorting the classroom out. Children love to help, so really getting them to wash all the plastic toys wasn't for me, it was for them...! They learned about responsibility, taking care of their belongings, hygiene, plus they were outside enjoying the glorious weather. That's how I'm spinning it anyway! We had a big old sort out of all the drawers and the resource cupboard and I felt so bad for them when we discovered a bunch of toys that I didn't know were in there so hadn't been used! They got a good playing with this morning. If this was Toy Story those toys would be over the moon.

Also, in an effort to build up the children's muscles as well as their independence, some lucky things were even given responsibility of ferrying some of my belongings to my new classroom for me! Everyone's a winner.

**Wednesday 21st July**

I was a bit annoyed that we weren't allowed to take PPA/ECT time this week as it's the final week, but I'm quite happy I didn't in the end because oh hello, the presents have started to roll in! I didn't think I'd be as lucky as Christmas but already there's a lot of love coming in! Initially, I was so excited to open them but that was soon replaced by such a huge, overwhelming wave of gratitude and joy when I started opening them. Amongst the chocolates and bottles of wine (very gratefully received!) there was a personalised bead bracelet that Katerina had made me herself, a small photo frame with a handwritten message from Benji along with my name in scrabble tiles and a personalised mug with matching coaster from Betty. Dale even bought me a Winnie the Witch book that I haven't got, and he'd written on the inside cover about how he knew I loved these stories and that I hadn't read this one! I was absolutely speechless and welled up at the amount of thought and effort these gorgeous children had put into my gifts! I am so lucky and I will keep all of these non-perishable gifts on my desk for as long as I am a teacher. The perishable ones have mostly already been devoured.

Some presents, on the other hand, are absolutely perfect for the charity shop. Some men's body spray (was this pulled out of your husband's wardrobe this morning?), some acne clearing face wash (perceptive but perhaps not exactly a present for someone you barely know) and some used lip balm (urgh!). Yes it's the thought that counts, but when your thought is "they have a lot of acne...", just put "thank you" in a card with a tic tac.

**Thursday 22nd July**

More presents and many, many, many hugs (from the children, not anyone's parents). It was Blake's last day today and funnily enough, despite the months of turmoil and stress and being kicked and spat at, no present or card came my way from that family. Dad just casually dropped off and picked up with a cheery "bye, have a nice summer!" Are you kidding me? Seriously, are you KIDDING me? I don't expect to be bought things, I'm not in this for presents and hadn't realised it would be a thing, though they are so wonderful to receive. But to not get a card or any form of recognition of the hell that that kid and I went through together... I absolutely can't believe it.

On the other hand, two parents asked me for a photograph with their child. They couldn't have done this in the morning when it wasn't a million degrees and I hadn't yet spent the day legging it round trying to herd 30 children around, mopping up accidents and sorting out arguments? They couldn't have asked me before school, when I wasn't sweaty and my freshly applied makeup was still matte and my hair was not yet frizzy? No. After school. The kids looked like they'd been through a war (today they decided to get fully inside the hedge in the outdoor area) and there they are, in a photograph that will probably go onto Instagram, with their hot, exhausted teacher. I'll remember this tomorrow and have a bit of a freshen up before we settle down for our end of the day story. I bet nobody asks tomorrow.

(Bed time: 10.15pm! This is what not teaching does to a person)

**Friday 23rd July**

Oh my goodness it's over. My first year of teaching is done! I don't know whether to laugh or cry. Do I sleep or party? I feel all the feelings right now. I had so many genuinely beautiful cards from parents and children, saying such wonderful, kind words about me being their child's teacher and how much I've helped them or how much they've loved this year. I'm so touched, not thinking about the data and the percentages and the statistics, but the intangible impact I've had on some of these families.

Teaching is so difficult and there have been many things that took me by surprise that placements at university don't teach you. It's not a profession that always feels very appreciative or kind, like when you're being told your Outstanding lesson still isn't good enough or that even though every child in your class has made better than expected progress their attainment levels still aren't good enough. There are some awful parents that think I could have pushed their child harder or not asked them gently to reflect on their actions after punching someone else in the face because it was in self-defence. However, there are some bloody glorious parents, who appreciate the crap out of me and like to show me, and some bloody glorious children who have given me such joy this year. Some moments of tearing my hair out, yes, and I've been far too involved in their bodily fluids for my liking, but their appreciation is just everything. Fabio was struggling with his behaviour this year because of some difficulties at home that he didn't quite know how to handle so I've been finding different ways of supporting him with his anger. He actually wrote in his card to me "thank you for listening to me". Wow. I openly and unashamedly wept at that.

I will never forget this first year or these first families who have taught me so much. I'm so incredibly proud of all of them, and myself. I'm so lucky to be starting my career in such a warm, supportive school with some incredible staff, and I owe a lot to TTA, who didn't want to get stuck with another newly qualified teacher but helped me so much anyway. It turns out, she's not so scary and I genuinely think that TAs are the nurses of education; they make the world of difference and they are integral to both pupils and teachers. I will be forever grateful to her and all the other TAs who are underpaid and overworked and generally have to deal with a lot of the rubbish stuff.

I suppose the moral of this story is to be exceptionally grateful for all of the thanks I get as a teacher. It's often overshadowed by criticism, constructive or otherwise, but I mustn't forget those little humans to whom my care, effort and teaching means the world. Even if they don't realise it means the world to them. It absolutely does.

One note, however, written by the parent of Rahul (who still just calls me Young), said in their understanding of English "you will be missing". I won't sleep for a week after this threat.

What a year.

# Acknowledgements

I have been wanting to write this book for a long time but never really had the confidence. I've always loved telling the stories of all the children I've taught and the parents that have to come with them and for the most part, my family have seemed to enjoy hearing them!

My husband was the one who made this all possible. He encouraged me to sit down and just start putting some ideas on an empty page and from there, it all just poured out! I will be forever grateful that I married someone who can be so unfailingly supportive, optimistic and encouraging, throughout the tantrums of getting stuck or thinking I'm not good enough. Thank you my love; it would never have happened without you. I also owe you a huge thank you for illustrating the book for me. I love your drawings and although you must have regretted agreeing to it, they finish off the exact vision I had in my head of how this book would look.

To my 'twin', my wonderful sister, confidant and biggest cheerleader. Thank you for proof reading a million times, even when I made the tiniest edit. You inspire me, love me and feel with me and I could not have done this without your words of wisdom and love. I also appreciate how silly you are because our childhood of being ridiculous together helped to shape the type of teacher I am!

My Mum is a selfless, kind, wonderful (shrinking) woman who has loved me and helped me through everything in my life. You feature largely in this book, as you do in my life, and I am so grateful for all the love and support you have always given me. Even when I was a teenager. Urgh. I will never be too old to want or need you! You consistently inspire and amaze me.

I need to thank my Dad for all his imparted wisdom and advice, without which I wouldn't be the semi-adult I am. I'm not sure I'll ever get to a point where I don't need you to help me with some DIY. I'm so grateful for everything you do for me and everything you have taught me.

I have some utterly wonderful friends and family who have been so supportive and excited for me to write this book and one in particular who has pushed me to keep creative time a prominent part of my life. No-one has told me I can't or that I shouldn't do it, and the belief that you all have in me has been more powerful than you can know. I'm so lucky to have such a vast support system of love and empowerment and joy.

I want to thank everyone I have ever worked with. You have either shown me the type of teacher I wanted or not wanted to be (!), and either way that has been so impactful. Teachers, teaching assistants, school caretakers, office staff and everyone else who works with children are generally hard-working, passionate, resilient beings who are often misrepresented, blamed or beaten down. To me, you are superheroes. I see you and I see your power in enhancing the holistic development of children in your care.

To the wonderful parents who have been inquisitive and supportive and worried and proud and glorious; thank you! You have one of the hardest jobs in the world and I have so much respect for what you do.

To the bellend parents; you are the worst. Be better.

Finally, all my heartfelt thanks goes to every single child I've ever taught. The strange, the genius, the dribbly, the aggressive, the chatty, the snarky, the hilarious, the anxious, the snotty, the stinky, the loud, the distractable, the quiet, the perseverant. You all taught me so much. I've laughed, I've cried, I've screamed, shouted and smiled. I've been proud, I've been annoyed, tired, lazy and energized. It's all because of you. I will never regret being a teacher. Thank you.

# Afterword

I, the teacher behind the pseudonym Felicity Youngwood, have been a teacher for over ten years. Amongst some other unrealistic goals, it was the overriding career that I always worked towards. I loved working with children and at university, was desperate to get out of the lectures and into placements. I wanted as much responsibility as the class teachers would be comfortable giving me and I threw myself into it.

Teaching always came relatively easily to me. I was always prepared, was able to have fun with the children but also laid down boundaries. I was relatively confident there. I didn't have much contact with children's parents during my three years studying for a teaching degree and this in no way prepared me for all the different characters I would meet when I had my own classes!

I am not too proud to say that first year of being a teacher was a bit of a shock! The overwhelming sense of responsibility for keeping thirty children alive, seeing the judging looks of parents who clearly thought I was too young to be teaching their children, having to be a teacher all day every day without being able to pass it back to their non-student class teacher! I learned so much in that first year, in no small part due to my TA, who in actual fact was not terrifying at all. The TAs I've worked with have all been incredible. They get paid so little and so much is expected of them; they always go above and beyond.

It often feels like teachers are up against it. We're expected to perform time and time again, we're inspected and observed and we're never good enough. There's always more to do, more to achieve, further to push the children and better statistics to provide. But parents are never all happy, management are often more focused on data than real life and those who aren't teachers get annoyed about the holidays we have. This book started as an idea to record all of the stories about children I had in my mindtank, but it evolved to wanting to advocate for them. Some teachers are lazy and rubbish, I'll give you that, but the majority will never stop pushing themselves to be better and give the children the absolute best education possible. We're in Poundland at weekend buying extra supplies that the school can't afford, we research in our spare time how to help those children we're just not reaching, we plan ridiculous activities that will help make learning fun and interactive.

I am hoping that anyone wanting to be, or is currently, a teacher will feel seen and validated. I hope that parents offer a little bit of empathy and that those who aren't teachers perhaps try to consider what the job entails before jumping to harsh conclusions.

I hope the stories in this book bring you some joy and/or some understanding. They are all true and they are all cherished memories.

Printed in Great Britain
by Amazon

24078495R00099